# A Song for Jeffrey

## Constance M. Foland

American Girl ™

Published by Pleasant Company Publications
©1999 by Constance M. Foland

Visit our Web site at **www.americangirl.com**

Printed in the United States of America.
First Edition
99 00 01 02 03 04 05 RRD 10 9 8 7 6 5 4 3 2 1

Editorial Development: Andrea Weiss, Michelle Watkins
Consultant: Mary Rack, Muscular Dystrophy Association
of Southwestern Wisconsin
Art Direction and Design: Kym Abrams
Production: Kendra Pulvermacher, Pat Tuchscherer
Cover Photograph: Wendy Popp
Cover Illustration: Jean Fujita

Library of Congress Cataloging-in-Publication Data
Foland, Constance M.
A song for Jeffrey / by Constance M. Foland.
p. cm. "AG fiction."
Summary: Lonely eleven-year-old Dodie meets Jeffrey,
who has muscular dystrophy, and discovers what it is like
to have a real friend, even as his condition worsens.
ISBN 1-56247-849-4    ISBN 1-56247-754-4 (pbk)
[1. Muscular dystrophy Fiction.  2. Physically handicapped Fiction.
3. Friendship Fiction.]  I. Title.
PZ7.F7267So   1999   [Fic]—dc21   99-29228   CIP

*To Dad*

# A Song for Jeffrey

# Chapter **One**

"**I**'ve spent my who-ole life, my whole life yer-r-nin'," Dodie crooned.

"Could you shut up for just one second?" Peter complained. "I am so sick of hearing you sing about that *yernin'*. What could an eleven-year-old possibly yearn for anyway?"

"Hah! What do you know," Dodie called out. She posed at the hallway mirror, holding an imaginary microphone up to her mouth and flicking her hair from one side to the other.

"Well, excuse me if you can't stand to tear yourself away from the mirror," Peter said, "but it's time to eat dinner."

Dodie sat down at the supper table. "You're just jealous because I'm going on TV and singing my song."

Peter rolled his eyes. "Yeah, right. Are you going to wear your Scouts beanie when you make your television debut?"

Dodie didn't understand her big brother, Peter. One day he did cool things, like help her hide her stupid Scouts hat so she wouldn't have to wear it anymore, and the next day he made fun of her, calling her a little fifth-grade brat. Peter used to be her best friend, but all that had changed since he started junior high.

"Well, I'm trying out for the school talent show tomorrow, then I'm going on TV to sing my song. Right, Daddy?"

"You can do anything you set your heart on doing, pumpkin. Where there's a will, there's a way."

She turned to her father and smiled. He was with them tonight on some sort of a trial basis. Their mother said he wasn't moving back in with them. He was just seeing how it would be if he visited and ate supper with them occasionally.

So far, so good. At least their father stayed put at the table instead of making his usual dash for the TV as soon as he had finished eating. That gave her mother less to complain about, so there was none of the usual arguing or slamming around of plates and silverware.

When her father turned away, Dodie opened wide and flashed Peter a mouthful of chewed meat loaf.

Peter groaned. "Mom, do I have to sit here and take this?"

"You may be excused."

"I need to be excused, too," Dodie said. "I have to rehearse." Then she quickly looked up at her father. "You'll still be here when I finish, won't you, Dad?"

"You bet."

Dodie sang her song over and over again, practicing in her mom's mirror. Peter had been teasing her that it sounded like a country-western love song, but she took that as a compliment. She just knew she'd be the only one at the school talent show tryout with something she made up herself.

She picked up a hairbrush and sang into it. ". . . And I've spent my who-ole life, tossin' and turnin'." She moved from the mirror to the closet.

"Mom? I need something sparkly for tomorrow. Do you have anything I can wear?"

"Dodie, don't you have Scouts tomorrow?"

"Oh, brother," Dodie mumbled into the dresses

and sweaters. "I can just see me now." Why did they have to keep reminding her of Scouts? It was bad enough that she had to wear that babyish uniform to school once a week. They couldn't possibly expect her to perform in it.

"I think I'm outgrowing my uniform, Mom."

"Mm-hmm," her mother muttered, lost behind her newspaper.

Digging deeper, Dodie found a feathery scarf and wrapped it around her neck. She rubbed it on her cheek and remembered a time once when her mother had carried her, wrapping the scarf around both of them. The scarf smelled now as it did then, like the powder of her mother's neck and the smoothness of her skin. Dodie took the scarf for good luck and sneaked past her mother, who was still engrossed in the news of the day.

"It's a little long, Dode. Wrap it around twice so you don't trip over it."

Dodie stopped in the doorway. She tossed the ends of the scarf over her shoulders and swished out of her mother's room.

The next day Dodie waited for her turn at the tryout. Only one person from each class was going to be chosen to perform in the show. She watched her classmate Brenda Hart shuffle across the stage in what was supposed to be a tap dance.

Dodie rolled her eyes and slid down into her seat. She knew she should have gone first so she wouldn't have to wait. It seemed her whole life consisted of waiting. Waiting to be older so she could do fun stuff like Peter did. Waiting for a best friend to come along so she wouldn't be alone all the time. Waiting for her parents to get back together. Dodie sighed and leaned her head into her hand.

"Dodie, shhh. I can't hear Brenda's shuffles," said Miss Platz. Miss Platz always directed the shows at Green Meadow School. She was the music teacher, and Dodie would have liked her class except that Miss Platz was so out of style. This year, they weren't just singing corny music, they were also playing it on the recorder. The only good part was that Dodie was learning how to read and write out music, which meant that she would soon be able to write down the songs she made up.

When her turn finally came, Dodie got up onstage and began to sing. But she had never sung with a real microphone before. Now her voice sounded different, a little too loud and echoey. Dodie tried to adjust by moving the microphone farther away from her mouth, but then her voice came out too low.

"Put the mike up closer," interrupted Miss Platz.

Dodie took a deep breath and began again. She tried her best to hit the high notes and make the long notes vibrate. But the song she'd been practicing for weeks, her very own original song, seemed to have disappeared into the empty auditorium. Dodie suddenly couldn't remember which parts she had sung and which she hadn't. She closed her eyes and squeaked out the last few lines.

Miss Platz smiled and looked over her half-glasses. She made a note on her clipboard.

"Uh, thanks, Dodie. We'll be announcing the winners this week."

Dodie sighed and left the stage.

# Chapter **Two**

Later that week, Dodie was crushed when her teacher, Miss Strawberry, announced that Brenda Hart would be representing the fifth grade at the talent show.

Dodie groaned and slid down into her seat. *How come I never get a chance? When is somebody going to recognize my talent?* Some of the girls walked over to Brenda and congratulated her. Nobody said anything to Dodie.

Even though the rest of the class was working on the math problem of the day, Dodie took out her writing journal. When Miss Strawberry asked her to put it away, she pretended she didn't hear.

Finally, the teacher came over to her desk and squatted down next to her. She looked up into Dodie's face.

"Are you all right?"

Dodie just stared straight ahead.

"If something's bothering you, you can talk to me about it, OK?"

Dodie still didn't say anything. Miss Strawberry stood up and turned to another student. Dodie looked down at her journal. One tear dropped onto the empty page. She quickly rubbed it away and shut the book.

When she got home from school, Dodie ran upstairs to her room and slammed the door. She threw her backpack down and kicked it. "It's not fair!" She picked up her recorder and blew into it as hard as she could. "*Fweeeeeeet!*"

She tossed all her pillows into a pile on her bed and started pounding on them. "It's not fair!" Slam. "I can't stand it!" Whack.

Finally, sweating, she stopped punching. She slumped down on the floor next to the bed. "Nothing ever goes right for me."

She found her school yearbook and turned to Brenda Hart's picture. She took out a pencil and drew a mustache on her face. She also drew some pointy cat-eye glasses. Then Dodie sighed and put the book down. She looked at herself in the mirror. "I don't get it. Is there something wrong with me? Is there a reason why everything I do gets ruined?"

She picked up the recorder and played the song she had tried to sing at the tryout. Then she sang part of it. It sounded fine. "So why couldn't I do that today?" she asked her reflection.

She put on her favorite sweatshirt and went to find her mother.

She knocked on her mother's door. "Mom? Are you having quiet time?" Sometimes Dodie's mother meditated. That is, she sat very still for a long time doing nothing. She said it helped her feel peaceful. Dodie tried to do it with her once, but it was so boring that she gave up after a few minutes.

"No, Dode. Come in."

"I don't think I'll ever sing again, Ma."

"No?" her mother asked. She was stretched out on her bed, absorbed in a novel.

"Yeah, I had my one chance today and I blew it." She lay down next to her mother.

"Oh, Dodie. I know how you feel. But it's not your only chance."

Dodie sniffled. "I tried so hard. I practiced every day. I knew that song by heart!"

"Well, what do you think went wrong?"

"I don't know. I guess I just got too nervous."

Dodie turned over and buried her head in one of her mother's pillows.

"Do you think you'd feel better if you washed your face and we went out for a walk?"

"I don't want to."

"What would you rather do? Stay home and feel sorry for yourself?"

"I'm not feeling sorry for myself!" Dodie snapped.

Her mother stroked her hair. "Oh no? Here, look."

They looked in the mirror together, mother behind daughter. Dodie's mom stretched her top lip all the way to one side of her mouth and curled her bottom lip toward the other side. At the same time, she closed one eye and rolled the other toward the sky. Dodie giggled and leaned back against her mother's chest.

They walked along, Dodie karate-chopping the tall grass at the edge of the road, her mother stopping occasionally to pick up a stray piece of litter.

They passed the row of mailboxes that belonged to Dodie's family and their three neighbors. Dodie stopped to look.

"Dad still has his name on our mailbox."

"Yup, I guess he does." Her mother kept walking.

"Do you think he'll take it off?"

"I don't know, Dode."

"Do you want him to?"

*If she says yes,* Dodie thought, *then she doesn't love him anymore. If she says no, that means she does.* Dodie had to guess about these things because her mother hardly ever talked to her about her father or their separation. In fact, lately her mother hardly talked at all. Mostly she walked around the house forgetting things and mumbling to herself.

Her mother sighed. "I don't know, Dode."

"That's what you always say, Mom."

"Well, that's the truth. I don't know if your father and I can be together without arguing all the time. We're taking time out to think about things."

Dodie didn't understand why they had to separate just to think, but she decided not to ask any more questions for the moment.

They walked along in silence.

At the end of the road, her mother pointed and said, "Look! Finally, somebody must be moving in." Carpenters had been fixing up the vacant house at the end of the block for the last few months.

Now movers were wheeling refrigerator-size boxes out of a big truck parked in front of the house. Dodie looked for signs of kids but saw none. No bicycles or balls. No skateboards or sleds.

Instead she saw a wheelchair. Maybe a grandparent lived with this family.

"I don't think they have kids," she said, sighing. "Rats." She was tired of playing alone and had been wishing for a best friend for a long time.

There were the girls at Scouts, of course. But they weren't much fun. Certainly not Dodie's idea of friends. The whole thing was a big bore. Making yarn dolls and carving soap figures just wasn't her thing. So mostly she hung around by herself, reading or making music that nobody seemed to want to hear.

A woman came down the steps of the house.

"Hi there, we're your neighbors!" Dodie's mother called out.

Dodie took a chance. "Do you have any kids?" she asked hopefully.

"I sure do. I have a boy about your age. He just turned eleven."

"Where is he? Can I meet him?"

"Well, he's inside getting ready. He has an art lesson this afternoon. But I'll tell him I met you. His name is Jeffrey."

Dodie got very excited. A new boy on her street. And an artist, no less! Just like her. She would invite him over that weekend.

"My name's Dodie. We live just over there, in the red house." Dodie pointed down the street. "He can come over any time he wants."

"That's nice of you to offer."

"Will he be in school tomorrow?" Dodie asked.

"Yes, I think he'll be there."

"I'm sure you'll see him then, Dodie," her mother said. She smiled and waved good-bye to their new neighbor. "Well, we'll let you get back to your moving now. See you soon."

Dodie was disappointed when nobody new got on the school bus the next morning. The bus driver didn't even stop at Jeffrey's house.

But when Dodie got to school, there he sat.

He looked enough like the other boys. He had short, wavy hair. He wore jeans, a black T-shirt, and high-tops. But one thing made him different. He sat in a wheelchair. It was the same one Dodie had seen yesterday.

Dodie stared at him all morning. She had never known anybody in a wheelchair, except at the hospital where her mother worked as a lab technician.

She wondered about him. Could he move his legs? She knew he could move his arms because she saw him write and draw. Was he born that way?

How did he take a bath? How did he get dressed? Did his legs hurt? How did they—?

"Why are you staring at me?" Jeffrey suddenly asked from his spot near the front of the classroom.

"I wasn't. I was just thinking about sharpening my pencil." She pointed to the sharpener on the wall behind him.

Dodie looked away. She knew all the kids were staring at her now, just as they had been looking at Jeffrey earlier. Her face was on fire. She yanked a book out of her desk and flipped it open. She pretended to read, but the words melted together before her eyes.

# Chapter **Three**

**A**t home Dodie lay on her bed thinking about Jeffrey. How could he embarrass her like that in front of everybody? He must have thought she was a big idiot for staring at him for so long. But she hadn't meant it to be rude. And she wasn't the only one who'd been staring. All the other kids had, too. Miss Strawberry had introduced Jeffrey like he was just another regular kid. They never even discussed why he was in a wheelchair. Dodie couldn't help it—she was curious.

After a few minutes she got up and wandered around the room. The house felt lonely and cold. She turned the radio on, listened to one song, then snapped it off. Even music didn't cheer her up today.

Her mother was still at work. Peter was supposed to be in charge of Dodie, but she didn't know where he was. Probably in his room in the basement, reading wrestling magazines or watching TV. She decided to try to talk to him anyway.

As she walked downstairs, her eyes adjusted to the dim light. Some bedroom, she thought. It was more like a cave. Peter was on his bed reading a magazine and stuffing his face with potato chips.

"Hi, Pete."

He didn't look up.

"Can I have some chips?" she asked.

He passed the bag to her without saying anything. Dodie took out a handful and started talking. "You know, there's a new kid who moved into the Haywards' old house."

"Mm-hmm."

"I met him today."

"Hmm." Peter turned a page.

Dodie flicked the back of his magazine.

"What do you want?" he said, getting irritated.

"You wanna make a fort under the pine trees?"

"No."

"You wanna do the Oscar Mayer bologna thing on the phone?"

"Not really."

"What about hitting baseballs? I'll catch first," Dodie offered. She didn't even like baseball. She especially hated chasing the ball around. Sometimes Peter hit it really far.

Peter sighed. "I'm busy right now. I'm trying to read this."

"Oh, Mr. Big Man, Mr. Junior High School." Dodie flung the bag of chips at him. "Here, eat some more grease. Add to your pimple collection."

Peter looked at her and shook his head.

She stormed up the stairs.

Dodie went into her mother's room and got out the phone book. She selected a number at random and dialed it.

She cleared her throat and tried to make it sound deeper. "Is this Mrs. Adams? Mrs. Stanley Adams?"

"Yes. I'm not interested in buying anything right now, though. Thank you."

"Oh, I'm not selling anything, Mrs. Adams. I'm calling to make you the winner of a case of Oscar Mayer bologna. All you have to do is sing the Oscar Mayer bologna song. Can you do that?"

"Right now? Sing it right now?"

"Yes. You're on."

Mrs. Adams started to sing, and Dodie sighed. It didn't seem as funny now with nobody listening on the other end, making gross noises and trying not to crack up.

When Mrs. Adams had finished, Dodie congratulated her and said good-bye.

"Wait, aren't you going to take my address down so you know where to send the bologna?"

Dodie had forgotten this part. "Oh. Well, we have that in our computer files already. You should receive the bologna within four to six weeks. Bye!"

She sighed and hung up. Things just weren't as much fun alone. Peter used to love making crank calls. He was really good at them, too. Especially if the person on the other end heard strange noises and asked about them. Peter would say they were just noises from the recording studio or the bologna factory. The people usually believed him, too.

But Peter was too busy for Dodie now.

She looked at the clock. Four-thirty. Her father sometimes got home from work around this time. She decided to go into her mom's room and call him.

"Hi, Dad."

"Hi, Dodie. What's up?"

"Oh, nothing. I was just calling to talk."

"Oh, I see. What's new?"

"Well, you remember that new boy, Jeffrey, I told you about?"

"Now, which one is he?"

"The one who moved in on our street. I told you about him yesterday, remember?"

Her father didn't say anything.

"Dad? Are you there?"

Dodie heard papers rustling in the background. "What? Oh, yeah, sure. I'm listening."

"Well, I met him and he doesn't want to be friends with me."

"Maybe he's just shy."

"He isn't shy. He just doesn't like me."

"Well, there are plenty of other fish in the sea, Dode."

"But you don't understand. I wanted to be friends with *him*. There isn't anybody else to hang out with around here."

"Oh, Dodie. It's not the end of the world."

"But it's important!"

"You always think that. Things pass. Let me ask you this. Can you remember what you wanted so badly for Christmas last year?"

Dodie thought about it. "No. Why?"

"See? At the time you thought it was the most important thing in the world, and now you can't even remember what it was."

"This isn't Christmas. This is now. And there's nothing to do."

"Maybe you could take up a hobby of some kind. Aren't you making those yarn dolls in Scouts anymore?"

Dodie sighed. "Never mind. I have to hang up."

"Wait, listen. Aside from all that, how are you doing? Is everything OK?"

"Yeah, I'm OK."

"You keeping your spirits up?"

"Yeah."

"Listen, no matter how bad things get, you have to stay determined. Don't let life get you down. When one door closes, a window opens. There's light—"

*—at the end of the tunnel.* Dodie knew what came next. She could have finished it herself. She had heard her father say it sixty kabillion times before.

Dodie waited till he finally ran out of things to say.

"All right, Dad. I'll try to look on the bright side."

"That's my girl. Any time you want to talk, you just call me, you hear?"

"Yeah, I hear."

"Don't you worry. Everything will be OK. Worrying never solved anybody's problems. If I had a dime for every time I worried—"

"I know. You'd be a millionaire. I have to get off the phone now, Dad. I'll see you."

"Okey-dokey. Take care."

Dodie went back to her room. But she was worried that everything would not be OK. She squeezed her pillow over her head and tried not to think about it.

# Chapter **Four**

For a long time, Dodie stayed away from Jeffrey. But she spied on him when he couldn't see her. At lunchtime he ate with some of the boys. And at recess, occasionally, one of the kids walked next to him as he wheeled out of the cafeteria, down the ramp, and onto the playground. But mostly he sat outside alone. Just like her.

Dodie wondered if he felt lonely, like she did, or if he really just liked being by himself. So many times she had wanted to talk to him, but after feeling so stupid that first day, she just didn't know what to say.

Dodie noticed that Jeffrey carried his sketch pad with him almost everywhere he went. Just like she carried her recorder and a little notebook. On the playground, he would sit drawing. Occasionally Miss Strawberry would walk over to him and lean down to see what he was working on. When he finished a picture, sometimes he would give it to Miss Strawberry, and she would hang it up on the bulletin board.

He drew beautiful scenes. Usually they were made-up, faraway places, like fairy worlds. Magical places where animals walked and talked. He drew one picture of an imaginary land covered in fog. It was lit up by the moon and stars, and it had a sea that floated into the distance. Tiny white waves splashed in the water, rolling away to nowhere. Dodie liked that picture best of all, but she never told Jeffrey that.

This morning, Dodie noticed, Jeffrey was late getting to the auditorium for the talent show. She didn't pay much attention to that, though, because she was in a rotten mood. She wasn't looking forward to watching Brenda tap-dance.

In the auditorium, Dodie sat at the end of a row. Just as the show was about to begin, Jeffrey wheeled in and stopped his chair next to her seat. She looked at him and half-smiled but didn't say anything.

Up onstage, Brenda acted like a real ham. She wore a hat with a wide brim and a black bow around the top of it. It must have been her father's hat, because it kept slipping off to one side, covering up her left eye. She shook a cane in the air, then stood it on the floor and shuffled around it. Dodie could hardly stand to watch.

But the other kids loved it. They clapped along with the music when Brenda kicked high and as the drums tapped out a loud, steady beat. Dodie imagined how it would feel to be up there, to have everybody clapping along with her. And after the show, everyone would want to talk to her and be her friend. Dodie remembered back to the day at the tryout. She slumped down into her seat. *If only,* she thought. *If only I had gotten it right.*

Finally Brenda danced off, lifting her hat high and waving it in the air. Dodie sighed and rolled her eyes.

Soon the kids were filing out. Dodie stood up, stretched, and stepped out into the aisle. Next to her, Jeffrey struggled with his wheels and tried to push himself up the aisle toward the exit. Dodie looked around for Jeffrey's helper. Miss Strawberry had assigned him a "buddy" for times like these, when they were out of the classroom, but his buddy was absent today.

Dodie called after her teacher to remind her about Jeffrey, but the din in the auditorium drowned her out. Miss Strawberry was already halfway up the aisle, her noisy students trailing behind her.

Dodie turned back to Jeffrey. His face was starting to turn red. She shrugged her shoulders and slowly followed the others. After a moment, she turned to look back. One part of her wanted to help him. But he was not the kind of kid who liked help. He sometimes got mad when Miss Strawberry tried to maneuver his chair in a certain direction or brought books or supplies over to him instead of letting him try to get them himself. He hardly ever let his buddy help him, except in the cafeteria line, where he had a hard time reaching the food.

Dodie walked slowly back down the aisle.

"Eh-hem," she said.

Jeffrey looked up. "Oh, hi."

"Looks like you're stuck, maybe."

"No, I don't think so. I just have to get myself moving." He tried to push again, but Dodie knew he wasn't going anywhere.

"You sure you're in the right gear?" Dodie asked.

"What are you talking about? This thing doesn't have gears."

"It was just a joke."

"Ha ha."

"Do you want me to give you a little push to get you started?" She reached toward the handles of his chair.

"No!" His shout made her jump.

"Sor-*ry*!" Dodie snapped back. "I was only trying to help."

"I'll do it myself. I'm just . . . resting."

Dodie shrugged and put her hands in her pockets. She dug her toe into a piece of gum stuck to the floor. By now, the only sounds in the big hall were of kids laughing and racing around behind the stage curtain.

Jeffrey struggled again with the wheels, then punched the arms of the chair. "I need to get motorized."

"Come on," Dodie said. "We have to go. I know you don't want help, but you can't get up this aisle by yourself." She grabbed the handles of his chair. "What do you expect me to do—leave you here?"

Jeffrey sighed.

She didn't wait for an answer. She began pushing him toward the door.

"Why don't you have a motor on this thing?"

"I need to use my arms. It keeps me strong."

They walked along in silence until Dodie blurted out, "So what's wrong with you that you're in a wheelchair, anyway?"

"I have a muscle disease."

"Oh. So does it hurt or anything?"

"Sometimes. But mostly it's just hard to move around."

Suddenly Jeffrey took control of the wheels again, causing Dodie to stop short and bump into him.

"Hey! What are you doing? You almost tripped me, you know."

"You can stop pushing now."

"Well, thanks for telling me."

"Sorry."

"Whatever. Well, I guess you don't need any more help." She began to walk away.

After a minute, Jeffrey called after her. "Hey, Dodie. Wait."

She turned around. "What?"

Jeffrey caught up to her. "Thanks for helping me."

"Yeah. Well. You're welcome."

Dodie continued to walk alongside Jeffrey. But neither one of them said anything the rest of the way back to class.

# Chapter **Five**

**A**t lunchtime, Jeffrey wheeled himself up next to Dodie, where she sat at the end of a long table in the cafeteria. Everybody was talking about the talent show, making jokes and giggling about who did what and how good they were.

Dodie scooted away from them as far down as she could. "Stupid talent show," she mumbled to no one in particular.

Jeffrey rolled his eyes.

"What?" she said. "I could have done better than all of them."

"So why didn't you try out?"

"I did. I just . . . well . . . I must not have been

feeling well that day because I didn't do so great."

"What's your talent?"

"I'm a singer, and sometimes I make up my own songs. My father says someday I'll be good enough to go on TV."

"Oh, really?"

"Yup. Maybe when I get older. What kinds of talents do you have?"

Jeffrey smiled. "My mother says I'm really good at painting and drawing."

"No, I mean the kind of talent you could perform in a show."

Jeffrey's smile flattened. He looked down.

"I mean," Dodie stammered, "it's just that, well, in a talent show you're supposed to actually *do* something, aren't you?"

"Yeah, I guess . . ." Jeffrey didn't look up.

"So, what are you eating?" Dodie said quickly, changing the subject.

"Just bologna with mustard."

"You want some of my chips?" she offered.

"No thanks."

"Are you on a special diet or anything?"

"Why should I be? Are you?"

"No. I just thought that maybe, because—I don't know. I was just asking, that's all." Dodie slumped in her chair.

"I eat whatever I want to. That is, whatever my mom lets me eat," Jeffrey said.

"Oh. I usually make my own lunch," Dodie said. "Do you?"

"Nope. I'm too lazy."

"Could you if you wanted to, though?"

"You mean, would my mother let me?"

"No. I mean, could you do it?"

"Dodie, I'm not mentally retarded!"

"I didn't say you were! I was just trying to make conversation."

"Just like you were trying to make conversation about me not being able to be in the talent show?"

"Why do you keep making me feel so stupid?!" Dodie asked. "You have some comment to make about everything I say."

"Well, you talk to me like I'm a baby. You act like I can't do anything. How do you think that makes me feel?"

Dodie stopped chewing.

"I wasn't trying to make you feel stupid. I'm just curious. Wouldn't you be if you saw somebody in a wheelchair?"

"Just because I'm in a wheelchair doesn't mean I'm not a regular kid. I'm in school just like you, aren't I?"

"Yeah, but . . ."

"I have to do homework and take tests and go to stupid assemblies just like you, don't I?"

Dodie laughed. "You don't like assemblies?"

"No. Not the stupid ones. And I have a lot of things I can't stand and a lot of things I love, just like anybody else."

"But what about being handicapped?"

"We don't call it that anymore. We call it being 'physically challenged.'"

"What does that mean?"

"The same as handicapped, I guess."

"What exactly is your challenge?"

"I have muscular dystrophy. I can't move my legs."

"Were you born that way?"

"Well, I was born with the disease, but I didn't start getting any of the symptoms until a couple of years ago. That's when I began having trouble breathing and moving my legs."

"Is there anything that can help it?"

"I go to physical therapy at a special clinic. That's why we moved to our new house. It's closer."

"What's therapy like?"

"It's not bad. I exercise in the water."

"So you could get better, couldn't you? My father says 'practice makes perfect.'"

"Boy, you sure ask a lot of questions. What are you doing, writing a book or something?"

"My father says the best way to make friends with someone is to ask questions about the person's life. I'm just trying to be nice."

"But all you want to know about is what's wrong with me and why I'm in a wheelchair. I can do a lot of other things, you know. Watch."

Jeffrey picked up a raisin and, with a flick of his wrist, threw it high into the air. Then he caught it in his mouth. "How's that for a talent?"

Dodie tried to do the same thing. The raisin missed by a mile.

"I bet you can't do one out of five," Jeffrey challenged Dodie.

"I bet I can."

Now the rest of the kids looked on.

Dodie tried five more times. Every time she missed. Raisins hit her in the chin and in the eye and bounced off the table, but not one found its way into her mouth.

"I won!" Jeffrey said triumphantly. Everyone clapped and cheered.

Dodie's face turned red. "I wasn't concentrating. And it's a stupid game, if you ask me."

"You're just mad because you couldn't do it."

"Am not."

"Are so."

"Shut up!"

"*You* shut up!"

Dodie narrowed her eyes at Jeffrey. "Well, the only reason you won is because . . . because I *let* you win."

Then she picked up her tray and left the table.

# Chapter **Six**

**A**fter school that afternoon, Dodie got on the bus and walked to the back where the junior high kids were sitting. Peter sat wedged in between two of his friends. The three of them huddled together over a mini computer game.

"Hi, Pete."

Her brother looked up. "Oh, hi." He continued laughing and talking with his friends. Dodie sat in the seat in front of them.

"What are you guys playing?" she said, twisting herself around to look over the back of the seat.

Peter mumbled, "Just a baseball game." He didn't look up.

"You think I could play?"

"Dodie . . ."

"What?"

"It's a guys' game."

"What's that supposed to mean?"

Peter's friend nudged him. "You're up, Pete."

Now Dodie stood on her knees, leaning over the seat. "Let me just try."

Peter's friend looked at him. "Come on, Pete, we don't have all day."

"Dodie," Peter hissed, "why don't you go sit with the little kids and leave us alone?"

Dodie slumped down. "Yeah, sure. I'll just go sit with the little kids," she mumbled to herself.

Peter stood up and leaned over the seat. "Come on, don't be such a baby."

Dodie got up and moved to the front of the bus. She flung herself into a seat and stared out the window.

A few minutes later, the bus reached their corner. Usually she waited for Peter, but today Dodie walked down the street alone.

Soon Peter caught up and walked next to her.

She stared straight ahead. "I'm surprised you would allow yourself to walk with a baby," she said coldly.

Peter didn't say anything.

"Mr. Big Head and his cool friends."

Peter kept walking.

"Too cool for words, I guess," she continued.

Suddenly Peter stopped and turned toward Dodie. "You always have to get your own way, don't you? If something doesn't go the way you want it to, you just get mad and sulk, right? Well, I'm tired of it. I have to babysit you almost every day now that Mom and Dad . . ." Peter trailed off. "The least I can do is have some fun with my own friends on the bus."

"Well, I can't help it if I'm not old enough to stay home alone."

"Yeah, well, I'd be out playing baseball every day if I didn't have to watch you."

"It's not my fault that Mom started working extra hours at the hospital. What do you want me to do about it?"

"Why don't you give me a break once in a while and try sitting with your own friends on the bus?"

Dodie opened her mouth to complain, but nothing came out. She shifted from one foot to the other and looked down.

*I thought you were my friend,* she wanted to say, but Peter had already walked away.

Instead of going inside, Dodie plopped down under the willow tree in the yard. She saw Peter through the kitchen window. He stood at the sink, washing dishes.

She pulled at the grass growing under the tree. Was it true what Peter said? That she sulked if she didn't get her own way?

Something made her think back to lunch. Her stomach sank when she remembered what she had said to Jeffrey when he beat her at the raisin game. She leaned against the tree and thought about it for a long time.

Finally she went inside to help Peter dry the dishes. After a few minutes of silence she said, "I didn't know you minded so much about baby-sitting me."

Peter shrugged.

"But we have fun sometimes," she said.

"Yeah, sometimes."

"But it's more fun with kids in junior high, right?"

"It's just different."

Dodie wiped a plate and stacked it with the others. She looked at her big brother. "What if I join the after-school program?"

"You hate after-school."

"Well, I won't go every day. Maybe just twice a week."

"Suit yourself."

"OK. I'll ask Mom to sign me up."

"Really?"

"Why not? Then you can play baseball, and maybe I can go to the drama club."

"What are you going to tell Mom if she asks why you suddenly changed your mind?"

Dodie grinned. "I'll just tell her I'm bored here, watching you pick your pimples all the time."

# Chapter **Seven**

**T**he next morning at school, Dodie walked over to where Jeffrey was sitting.

As usual, he was drawing.

She took out a box of raisins and placed it on his desk. "I challenge you to a rematch."

Jeffrey continued to draw. "Yeah, right. Just so you can let me win?"

"No, for real."

"I don't want to play."

For a minute Dodie didn't say anything. Then she sighed. "Yeah, I guess I wouldn't want to play with me either."

Jeffrey looked up.

"My brother says I have a mean temper. That if I don't get my own way, I sulk."

Jeffrey shrugged.

"I didn't really let you win yesterday."

Jeffrey smiled. "No kidding."

"I hate to lose, don't you?"

"I don't love it, that's for sure."

Dodie opened the box and shook out a handful of raisins. "Come on. Best two out of three."

The next week, Jeffrey invited Dodie to his house. She walked there after school. When she arrived, his mother led her through the front door, up the ramp, and into the living room.

Dodie looked around and noticed railings running along all the walls. She walked down an extra-wide hallway, where her steps echoed loudly on the wooden floor. In Dodie's house, rugs covered every floor but the one in the kitchen. In Jeffrey's house, the floors were all bare. Dodie guessed it must be easier to wheel around on wood than on carpeting. She noticed, too, that the rooms seemed emptier. Less furniture to bump into, she figured. When they walked past the bathroom, Dodie stopped short. What about *that*? She had never thought about that before. How did he—?

"Anything wrong?" Jeffrey's mother asked.

Dodie bent down quickly. "Just tying my shoe." Pretending to fix her laces, she stole a look inside the bathroom but didn't notice anything unusual.

"Here we are," Jeffrey's mother sang out as they entered a large room. The inside was as bright as the day was outside. She looked up to see a huge window in the ceiling. Jeffrey sat off to one side, painting.

"That window is giant," Dodie said. "I've never seen a window that big in a ceiling."

"It's a skylight. See how the sun comes in? I can paint better in here."

"Is this your bedroom?"

"No. It's my art studio. My parents had it all fixed up for me."

Dodie looked around. Except for the window, everything in the room seemed . . . well, short. Paints of every color lined the shelves of one wall, but no shelf was higher than her shoulder. Pictures were tacked up all over the room. An unfinished painting stood on an easel. Dodie walked over to get a better look at it.

Then she glanced around, looking for some place to sit.

"There's a chair in the next room," Jeffrey told her. "You can go get it if you want."

Dodie brought the chair in. "So this is what you do after school?"

"Yeah. Some days. What do you do?"

"Not much. Mostly I sing and play my recorder. And I might be joining the after-school program."

"Do you want to paint something?"

"Sure."

He gave her a sheet of paper, a few brushes, and a tray of watercolors. She mixed some with water and thought about what to make. Finally she picked up a brush and poked at the whiteness. She jabbed again and again. Pretty soon she had covered the paper with specks and splotches.

"Looks like mud splashed on my paper," Dodie grumbled. She tore it up and threw it away.

Jeffrey looked up from his painting and frowned. "What's wrong?"

"I don't know. I can't do it. I stink at painting."

"No you don't. It just takes practice. Like singing. You said you're a singer, right?"

"Yeah, but that's different."

"Well, it takes time. When I was first learning, my mom taught me that whatever I painted was OK. Even if I thought it was junky. She says, 'We don't make mistakes, we just have learning experiences.'" Jeffrey pointed his finger down his throat and pretended to gag.

Dodie laughed.

"Here. Try it again," Jeffrey said, handing her another piece of paper. "You know what I do sometimes? I start out slowly, not knowing what I want to paint. But the next thing I know, I'm making lines and circles and it doesn't even matter what I'm painting. Try it. Don't even think about what it's supposed to be. Just paint whatever you're feeling."

"How can you paint *feelings,* Jeffrey?"

"Well, when you sing, you don't just sing the notes, do you? You put feelings into them. Right?"

Dodie thought of how she crooned the notes when she sang her country-western song. "Oh, I get it. Do you like to sing?" she asked.

"No. I can't carry a tune. I wanted to be in chorus once at school, but I flunked the tryout."

"Flunked?"

"Yeah, the music teacher told me to stick to art."

"Hmm. I can't imagine not singing."

Dodie tried to paint the way Jeffrey said. Soon a house appeared. With people inside. Stick figures for heads and dots for eyes. Slinkies for hair.

She held up the picture for Jeffrey to see. "Well, it's a start," she giggled.

Jeffrey wheeled over to get a better look. "There's more paper if you want to paint anything else."

Dodie excused herself to go to the bathroom.

Once inside, she locked the door. Then she looked all around, hoping to find the answer to her question. The bathroom looked very much like hers at home. No special equipment. No mechanical seat to hoist Jeffrey up and down. The toilet was the same size. The sink was the same, too. She peeked behind the shower curtain. Special bars ran along the walls of the tub. Well, that explained how he bathed. But what about . . . ? Maybe Jeffrey had a special toilet in his room. Her mother might know. She would have to ask later.

When she got back to Jeffrey's studio, Dodie looked at him very carefully. She wasn't sure what she was expecting to see—a miniature toilet under his wheelchair? A bag connected to his leg?

She just stared. "Jeffrey? Can I ask you a question?"

"Yeah?"

As soon as he looked up, her face got hot. "I, uh, I was just wondering . . ."

"Yeah?"

"Well, it's kind of personal . . ."

"Yeah?"

"Well, um . . . Do you want to come out with my father and me this Saturday?" Dodie blurted out. It was the only thing she could think of to say.

"Saturday? What time? I have to go to physical

therapy. Remember that special clinic I was telling you about?"

"Oh yeah."

"I go in the morning."

"Well, that's OK. My father won't be getting here until one o'clock."

"Where's he coming from? Doesn't he live with you?"

She would have to tell him sooner or later. "Well, no, not right now. My mom and dad are separated."

"Oh, that's too bad."

"Yeah, but it's probably not for long, though."

"So when do you see him? Only on Saturdays?"

"Mostly. He doesn't come every Saturday. Sometimes he's too busy."

"Working?"

"Yeah. I guess so."

"On a Saturday?"

Dodie felt her stomach tighten. She sucked in some air and let it out quietly. When the tight feeling passed, she said, "Well, he's a busy man. And he has a lot on his mind."

"Yeah. My dad used to work a lot, too. Now he stays home more to help me."

"Anyway, do you want to come or not?"

"I don't know. Last week I had to lie down for the whole day after therapy."

"The whole day?" Dodie rolled her eyes. "Wow."

"Yeah, I know. It's not much fun. But I'll ask my mom, OK?"

"OK. You can tell me at school tomorrow."

Dodie took another sheet of paper and quickly wrote out her name in big block letters. Then she decorated it, making each letter different. When she finished, she painted one for Jeffrey, making each of his letters unique, too. She showed it to him, and he tacked it up next to his easel.

"I better get going. Can I take this home?" she said, holding up the one of her own name.

"Yeah, but make sure it dries so it doesn't get smudgy."

"OK. Thanks."

"What about this one?" Jeffrey asked, holding up her picture of the house full of stick figures.

"Nah. That one's a present for you."

# Chapter **Eight**

"**M**om? I invited Jeffrey to come with me and Dad this weekend," Dodie said, hopping up onto her mother's bed.

"Does your father know?"

"Well, no, I haven't actually asked him yet."

"Don't you think that might be a good idea?"

"Yeah, but would you talk to him for me? Please?"

"Why don't you want to ask him yourself?"

"Whenever I call him, he's too busy to listen."

"Hmm."

"He'll listen to you, won't he, Mom?"

Her mother leafed through a magazine.

"Ma? Now *you're* not listening!"

"Yes I am, sweetie. Your father, well . . . he has a lot going on right now."

Dodie noticed a change in her mother's voice. She didn't sound mad, exactly. But she didn't sound happy either.

"Mom? Are you sad that Daddy doesn't live here anymore?"

Her mother didn't answer.

"Ma?"

"It's a hard question, Dode."

"But Mom, we never talk about this stuff. I know you and Dad used to fight a lot. But you never tell me what's going on now. And neither does he. All he ever says is 'keep your chin up' and 'look on the bright side.'"

Her mother looked down. "Maybe we could talk about this another time."

"Yeah, right." Dodie knew they never would.

Her mother sighed. "OK, OK, I'll call your father tonight. How's that?"

"Thanks."

Later that evening, Dodie was walking past her mother's room when she overheard her talking on the phone. Actually, her mom was scream-whispering—that's when she talked in a whisper, but loud. Dodie knew she was talking to her father. The two of them used to fight that way sometimes when he still lived at home. They would close their bedroom door and try not to yell.

"What do you mean, what they don't know won't hurt them? You've got to be kidding!" Her mother's voice filtered through the closed door. She said nothing for a few seconds. Then, in a somewhat calmer voice, "Look. I know we agreed not to drag them into our problems, but they keep asking questions."

Dodie took a deep breath. Her parents were fighting about her and Peter.

"She'll worry less if we talk about it!"

Her parents didn't want her to worry? How could they expect her not to?

"Listen. You and I obviously have different ways of doing things, especially when it comes to them," her mother continued in a low voice.

Dodie sighed. Once again her parents couldn't agree. Not even about what to tell their own kids.

"Why don't we just tell them that you need your space? That you never lived on your own and that you need to now?" Her mother paused. Then she said, "Well, I know they might not understand. I don't really understand it myself, frankly."

Whatever he answered did not sit well with her, because she started shouting again. "All right, then, fine! Fine!"

Dodie didn't want to hear any more. She just wanted her parents to stop. She rapped loudly at her mother's door and burst in without waiting for an answer. "Mom? Oh." She tried to look surprised. "I didn't really know you were on the phone."

Her mother held the receiver out to Dodie. "Here. It's your father."

Dodie asked her dad about Saturday and got off the phone as fast as she could.

Later, Dodie went down to Peter's room. He was standing in front of the mirror, flexing his muscles.

"You been working out again?" she asked.

"Yeah, can you tell?" Peter looked hopeful.

"Oh, definitely," Dodie lied. "You probably went up a size in T-shirts. At least in the sleeves."

Peter smiled. "So what's up?"

"Nothing. Just taking a break from homework."

Peter leaned his face close to the mirror and inspected his upper lip.

"Thinking about shaving?" Dodie asked.

Peter blushed. "Nah, just checking." He walked away from the mirror and flopped down on his bed. Dodie picked up a bottle of cologne that was sitting on his dresser. She sniffed it.

"Eeew. Are you actually planning to wear this?"

"It smells good. You're just not sophisticated enough to appreciate it yet."

"Yeah, right."

She sat down in front of the mirror. "Hey, Pete?" She spoke to his reflection. "You know that time I wanted to go to camp, and Mom and Dad had that big fight about it?"

"Because Dad didn't want to spend the money? Yeah, I remember. He thought you would cry after the first night and want to come home."

"I wouldn't have, though."

"I know."

"And you know how you're always wanting to try out for the football team, and Mom says no and Dad thinks you should be able to?"

"Yeah? And?"

"Well, I was just wondering. Do you think maybe Daddy moved out because of us?"

Peter didn't say anything for a long time.

Dodie turned to face him. "Pete? I don't mean because of you. It's just that I heard them fighting on the phone before."

"About us?"

"Sort of. Dad's telling Mom he needs to live on his own. Do you think it's *us* he wants to get away from?"

"No, I don't think he left because of you and me."

"How do you know?"

"Because he still sees us a lot and calls all the time. Some kids' fathers leave and never come back. Never! Some kids don't even know who their fathers are."

Dodie sat next to Peter on the bed. They both stayed quiet for a long time. Finally she said, "You think you'll ever have kids?"

"Yeah, probably. You?"

"Yeah. But I'm never going to get married."

# Chapter **Nine**

**T**he next day during recess, Jeffrey called Dodie over to where he was sitting under the big tree.

"Look." He spun his chair around. On the back he had hung the picture that Dodie had painted of his name.

Dodie laughed. "Hey, that looks pretty good!" She felt proud to see her artwork displayed. She grabbed the back of Jeffrey's chair. "Wanna go for a ride?"

"What are you talking about? You know I don't like to be pushed," said Jeffrey.

"No, I'm talking about a *real* ride." She wheeled Jeffrey out onto the smooth blacktop path and started to run.

"You're crazy!" Jeffrey said, laughing.

Dodie pushed faster and faster, running past kids playing kickball. She cruised past the basketball court. She picked up speed near the monkey bars. Kids stopped to watch them as they sailed by.

Then she slowed down just a bit. "Close your eyes, Jeff. See if it feels like you're flying."

She looked down to see if Jeffrey had done as he was told. He squinched his eyes tight. "Hold on," Dodie said. "Here we go."

Dodie raced Jeffrey all over the playground. The wind blew through her hair. Her legs felt like springboards. More kids stopped to watch as Dodie and Jeffrey zoomed past. Finally she slowed down and pushed Jeffrey back under the shade of the tree. Then she collapsed on the ground, laughing.

"How'd you like that?"

He leaned his head back on his chair. "It was wild. For a minute I did feel like I was flying." His words came out soft and airy, like bubbles.

Dodie lay down and gazed up at the sky. "See? I knew you knew how to have fun."

Dodie got up early on Saturday morning. On weekends she liked to go treasure hunting in the woods behind her house. She usually found all kinds of neat things back there, like pinecones and bird feathers. Even if she found nothing, she had fun pretending she was out in the wilderness of the jungle. If she kept very still, she could hear a strange rustling in the leaves.

"Wsss, wsss." She shook the branches as she passed them. She growled, "Grrr." Then she crouched down and crawled on her hands and knees. She inched forward.

Something very near her hand stirred. She turned her head and saw what looked like a small rock. She knew it wasn't, though. It had straight edges and a checkered top. A turtle! She had to get it and go show it to Jeffrey. She picked it up and stroked its back. It answered her by sucking its head all the way into its shell.

She ran the whole way to Jeffrey's house, taking care not to squish her new treasure. When she got there, she found Jeffrey outside, waiting to get into his parents' van.

"Hi," she called out. "You on your way to physical therapy?"

"Yeah. What are you doing?"

She held out the turtle. "Look what I found."

"What is it? A stone?"

"No. It's a turtle. I brought him for you. I got him while I was on safari out back."

"Hey, Mom," Jeffrey called. "Look what Dodie brought me."

His mother walked over to the van.

"Hmm. A box turtle."

"I found him." Dodie smiled.

Jeffrey's mother lifted him into the backseat of the van. She arranged his legs and said, "We're on our way to Jeffrey's clinic, Dodie. Want to come along for the ride?"

Dodie stopped smiling. "Um, I don't know."

"It's only for a little while. If you want to, we can stop at your house and ask your mom if it's OK."

Dodie stayed glued to the driveway. "Is it like a hospital there?" Dodie pictured kids hooked up to machines, getting tests, and shuffling down hallways. She had seen the bald-headed children going for cancer treatment at her mother's hospital. She looked at Jeffrey, her face a question mark.

"No, you'll see. Believe me, if it was anything like a hospital, you couldn't get me out of bed this early to go there," joked Jeffrey.

"Well, OK. If you're sure it's all right." Dodie opened the van door and slid in next to Jeffrey.

"Wow, this is it?" They walked past a large gym where kids in wheelchairs were playing basketball.

"It's a rec center, too," Jeffrey explained as they made their way through the clinic.

Soon they reached the indoor pool. "I have to go get ready," Jeffrey said. He wheeled off toward the boys' locker room.

"Can I look around?" Dodie asked his mom.

"Sure."

Down a hallway, Dodie discovered several more rooms. In one, a bunch of kids were playing on a computer. In another, a Ping-Pong game was going on. Dodie watched for a while, tempted to join in. Then she peeked into the last room. There she saw three kids talking in a circle. They seemed to be arguing, but as she got closer, she could hear them joking with each other.

Two of the kids gestured and moved their wheelchairs from one place to another. One boy talked while the other two listened and nodded. They seemed to be doing this over and over again.

*It must be a skit,* Dodie thought. These kids were rehearsing some kind of a show. She watched them for a while longer and wondered why two of the kids in this group sat in wheelchairs and one was walking around. She would have to ask Jeffrey about that.

When she returned to the pool, Jeffrey was in the water. A young man was helping him do different exercises. *This must be his physical therapist,* Dodie thought to herself.

After a while, the therapist clapped Jeffrey lightly on the back and said, "OK, I think that's enough for today." He leaned toward Jeffrey with his arms outstretched, as if to lift Jeffrey up.

"I can get out myself," Jeffrey said.

"Remember what happened the last time," his mother cautioned.

Jeffrey placed his hands on the edge of the pool. "I feel stronger today."

But Jeffrey did not look strong. Dodie saw the strain on his face as he straightened his arms and tipped his body forward. He flopped partway onto the edge of the pool, his shoulder twisted under him. He tried to drag his lower body out of the water, but he wasn't getting anywhere.

Dodie got a tight feeling inside as she watched him. Her stomach pressed into her ribs, and her chest felt like it was caving in. Her whole body felt stiff. She suddenly remembered how she sometimes felt when she was trying to learn a new song but couldn't get the notes right. She would sing the song over and over till her throat hurt. And still her voice squeaked on the high notes, and still she stumbled over the words. That didn't always happen, just on bad days.

It looked to her like Jeffrey was having one of those bad days.

Dodie breathed a sigh of relief when Jeffrey's therapist finally squatted next to him and said, "Come on, kiddo, let me help you. That's what I get paid for."

On the way home, Dodie told Jeffrey about the kids she'd seen doing the skit.

"Oh, they must be rehearsing for the spring show."

"What's that?"

"Every year around this time, our clinic has a big party and a performance. Some of the kids put on skits for it."

"Are you in the show?"

"Nah. I don't like doing that kind of stuff. It's fun to watch, though."

"Do you have to be a patient here to be in it? I saw one kid in the group who, um, who—"

"Wasn't 'handicapped,' you mean? He's a friend of someone in the group. Everyone who wants to be in the show gets to pick a friend who isn't physically challenged to be in the show, too. Our instructors say it's good for building community awareness, or something like that."

"When's the show?"

"In about four weeks."

"Well, what about you and me? We could be in it together!"

"Nah."

"Why not? Come on, it'd be great. We could sing a song!"

"Sing a song about what?"

"Any song. I'll teach you one."

"No way. Remember? I told you, I flunked chorus. And besides, I don't like getting up there in front of all those people."

"Please?"

"No, Dodie. N-O spells *no*!"

"I know how to spell."

"Then maybe you don't know how to listen. I said I'm not interested."

Dodie glared at him. "All right. Fine."

They rode the rest of the way home in silence.

Dodie couldn't understand it. Why didn't he want to do the show? Couldn't he see how important it was to her? Was he her friend or wasn't he?

When they pulled up to her house, Dodie said to Jeffrey, "Are you coming with me and my dad later or not?"

Jeffrey hesitated. "I don't think so. I'm feeling kind of tired."

"Oh, I see."

Dodie got out of the car and watched Jeffrey and his mother drive away.

# Chapter **Ten**

**D**odie was quiet as she sat with her dad at lunch.

"What's the matter? Cat got your tongue?" her father joked.

"No. Just thinking, I guess."

"My little thinker. You always did have the wheels turning a million miles an hour. Once, when you were little—you had to be five or six—I walked past your room late at night and saw that you were still awake. I stopped and said, 'What are you doing awake still?' And you said, 'Just thinking.' And I said, 'About what?' And you said, 'Just figuring stuff out.' And I said, 'What's a little girl like you doing trying to figure stuff out? That's what daddies are for!' After that you drifted off to sleep. At least I think you did." Her father winked.

Dodie sighed. She had heard this story, like most of her father's stories, quite a few times before. But now she imagined herself as a little kid. She wished she could be small again so she could play all day long and let her parents do the worrying. Being eleven was so much more responsibility.

"I was supposed to bring my friend Jeffrey today, remember?"

"Yeah, you told me. What happened to him?"

"I don't know. We kind of had a fight, and . . . I think he changed his mind."

"That's a man's prerogative."

"I thought it was a *woman's* prerogative to change her mind, Dad. Anyway, I don't think he really wanted to come in the first place."

"Why not?"

"He doesn't like to do anything fun. All he likes to do is sit and draw." Dodie suddenly remembered pushing Jeffrey around and around the playground. He'd had fun then. So was she just sulking now, like her brother said she always did when she couldn't have her way?

"I wanted him to be in this really fun show with me, but he said he wouldn't do it. He won't even try singing. Can you believe it?"

"Remember what I always say: Let persistence wear down resistance."

"Believe me, it won't work. He totally refuses."

"Where there's a will, there's a way, Dode."

"Dad! Everything doesn't get solved with a saying, you know."

"Well, there is a solution to every problem."

Dodie couldn't stand it anymore. She shouted across the table, "Oh *yeah*? Well, how come you and Mom can't solve *your* problems, then?"

Her father's eyes opened wide. He glanced around the restaurant to see if people were staring at them. "That's a much more complicated situation, Dodie," he hissed. "That's two adults working on a marriage. You're talking about two kids playing dress-up in a school pageant."

"It isn't a *school*. It's a special kind of *clinic,* and you don't even know the difference."

"All I know is that you're making a mountain out of a molehill, Dodie. This isn't the end of the world."

Dodie's face burned. She gritted her teeth and dug her nails into the arm of her chair.

"I want to go home."

"You don't want to have an ice cream soda with your dad?"

Dodie loved ice cream sodas.

"I don't want an ice cream anything."

"Not even vanilla with chocolate soda?"

Her favorite. "No."

"Dode?"

Dodie didn't look up. She was busy unraveling the corner of the tablecloth.

"All right. I guess I'll take you home, then."

Dodie stared out the window for most of the ride home. Her father flipped from station to station on the radio, looking for a ball game to listen to. Dodie hated the noise. Her father had an old car that still had the kind of radio with a dial rather than an automatic-seek button. So not only was she blasted by the blare of each station as he turned past it, but she was bombarded by the static in between.

She tried to concentrate on other things. She planned the rest of her day. She would take a walk, then maybe go out in the woods again. She had been thinking lately of building a fort. Unlike the one she had built with Peter, this one would be her own secret. The only problem was that she didn't know how to build anything. Peter had done all of the construction after she had hunted up scraps of wood and nails. So while she loved the idea of having a secret hideout, she didn't know how to go about building it.

Her father had always said he'd help with whatever she needed. Yeah, right. Just like he had helped her with her problem with Jeffrey. She glanced over at him without turning her head. She could tell he was listening to the baseball game on the radio. He listened to sports more than he listened to anything or anybody else. He edged closer to the radio to tune it in more clearly. His eyes squinted as he tried to hear what was happening. He muttered something under his breath. He seemed to be far away. He almost seemed to be in another world. He seemed—

"Daddy! Look out!"

The car swerved to one side, then back again. Her father's hands gripped the wheel. Dodie flattened herself up against the seat and squinched her eyes shut automatically. Brakes screamed and the car came to a halt. Slowly, Dodie opened her eyes. She was still in one piece. So was her father. But they had just missed crashing into another car.

"Daddy! What were you doing? You weren't even paying attention. You almost got us killed!"

Her father tried to chuckle, but no sound came out of his mouth. His face had changed from a light tan to white. He pulled the car over to the side of the road.

"Oh, Dode, relax. I've never had an accident in my whole life," he said. But he didn't sound very relaxed.

"It's not just that. It's everything."

"What are you talking about?"

"You're always saying I can come to you with my problems, but then when I do, you don't even listen! You answer me with some stupid saying or proverb."

His mouth opened, but he didn't say anything.

"And whenever I call you," Dodie continued, "you're too busy to talk, or you just make jokes out of everything." Tears began slipping down her cheeks.

After a long silence, her father finally said, "I don't know what to say, Dodie."

Dodie didn't either. She couldn't believe she had already said what she had. Yet she felt strangely calm, like some loud buzzing that had been inside her for a long time had finally stopped. She sniffled and then resituated herself in her seat.

Her father undid his seat belt and reached out to hug her. "I'm really sorry, pumpkin. I don't know what I'd do if anything bad ever happened to you. I'd go crazy."

For the first time that afternoon, Dodie felt like smiling. "You already are crazy." She giggled.

Her father laughed, too, and buckled himself back in. "I'm glad you told me how you feel."

"Yeah, so am I," she said. "And I want to change

the radio station, too. From now on, I'm in charge of the music."

"No more baseball?"

Dodie had already found a song she liked, an oldie her mother sometimes played at home. "No more baseball. Don't you like this song?"

"Yeah, it's OK."

"It's one of Mom's favorites, you know." Dodie turned up the volume. "What do they mean by 'so many promises broken'?"

"I guess it's about love gone wrong."

"Oh. Like you and Mom?"

Her father didn't say anything, but this time Dodie knew he was listening.

"I guess now I'm talking too much," she said.

"That's OK. You understand a lot more than I thought you did."

"Grown-ups always think kids don't get what's going on."

"Is that right?"

"Yeah, Peter and I knew something was wrong even before you moved out. You and Mom fought all the time. I thought it was because we were grating on your nerves."

"Is that what you thought? Dodie, this doesn't have anything to do with you guys. You two are the best part of our lives."

"So then, you and Mom just don't love each other anymore?"

"Well, that's not exactly it either, Dode."

"Then what is it?"

"I guess we love each other, but we just can't seem to get along."

"Couldn't you try counseling? That's what they always say on the talk shows."

Her father shrugged. "I'm not very good at that kind of thing."

"But what if it worked?"

"I don't know. The truth is, I'm kind of used to being on my own now."

"You mean you like living in a motel room and eating takeout every night?"

"No. But I guess I like making my own decisions to come and go as I choose."

Dodie pictured her father getting in late at night and sleeping until eleven o'clock on Sunday mornings without her or Peter there to wake him.

"Well, that's OK. We do all right without you."

Her father blinked twice, and his cheek twitched.

"Oh, I don't mean it in a bad way, Dad. I just mean it's not the end of the world." She smiled over at him. "As you would say."

"Hmm. Not the end of the world, huh?"

Dodie turned up the radio again and started singing. Her father shook his head and kept driving.

When they turned onto her street, Dodie said, "Could you drop me off at Jeffrey's house? I have to tell him something."

"You got it, chief. Then maybe I'll go over and say hello to your mom."

"That would be nice. So, I'll see you next weekend, right?"

Her father nodded. Dodie hugged him before she got out of the car.

"And don't be a reckless driver."

"OK, I won't."

## Chapter **Eleven**

**D**odie walked around the side of Jeffrey's house to see if he was in the backyard. He was sitting there in the sun, wearing red shorts and a tank top. His legs, thick and white, poured out of his shorts like rising bread dough.

Until this morning at the pool, Dodie had never seen Jeffrey in anything but long pants. She had been surprised to discover that he didn't have skinny, bony legs. In fact, they were actually chubby. Now they spread out and squished against the sides of his wheelchair, his feet pushed into unlaced sneakers. Dodie didn't understand it. But then, there were a lot of things she didn't understand.

Dodie took a deep breath and swallowed hard. Suddenly she was afraid to talk to Jeffrey. What if he was still mad at her about the fight? What if he never wanted to speak to her again? Her mouth dried out, and she became very thirsty.

Her mind flashed back to a scene at her mother's hospital. The kids in the children's wing were sitting around watching TV or playing cards. One boy wheeled into the room and sat by the window. His legs hung in the same lifeless way that Jeffrey's did now. The boy's face was pale and skinny. He started to cry quietly, without saying a word. Finally he wheeled himself out of the room. Dodie's stomach had bloated with feelings. Her heart had ached for the boy. She wanted to run after him and ask him what was wrong. But in the end she sat there and did nothing.

Her mind flipped back to Jeffrey's yard. She thought about sneaking away, but it was too late. Jeffrey had already seen her.

"Hi. I'm back," she said, coming across the patio.

"So I see."

Dodie's eyebrows squinched together. Her face felt hot. "Do you think I could have some water?" she squeaked out. Her mouth was so dry, she could barely speak.

"Yeah. But could you get it out of the hose over there? It's kind of a pain for me to get back inside without my mother's help."

Dodie got her drink and splashed some water on her face to cool down. She walked back to the patio. Before she spoke, she took a deep breath. "I wanted to say I'm sorry for all the bad things I've ever said to you." She swallowed hard.

Jeffrey raised his eyebrows.

"And also that I really want to be in the talent show at your center, but I think I understand why you don't. And I still want you to come out with my father and me sometime for lunch."

While Dodie talked, she tried not to stare at Jeffrey's legs. But he caught her sneaking a peek. "What's the matter?" he said. "You never saw thighs before?"

Dodie turned redder than Jeffrey's shorts. "Well, it's just that you usually only wear long pants."

"Not in the sun. How could I ever get a tan?"

Dodie saw Jeffrey smiling.

"Hey, look all you want to. I'm no Arnold Schwarzenegger, but I do get hot, you know. Here, can you lift these up?" Jeffrey pointed to the adjustable levers on the wheelchair. "I want my legs to be straight out."

She knelt down and reached out to a lever on the

side of the chair. When she had finished, Jeffrey's legs were sticking straight out in front of him. She lay down in the grass.

"Jeffrey? How did you get to be like you are? In a wheelchair, I mean."

"I told you, remember? It's just something I was born with. It's called a genetic defect."

"Like being born deaf or blind?"

"Yeah, same kind of thing, I guess."

"Which would you rather be? Deaf, blind, or like you are?"

"I don't know. I never had those other things. Which would you rather be?"

"Blind. No, deaf. No . . . blind. Because if I were deaf I wouldn't be able to sing."

Jeffrey rolled his eyes. "Deaf people can use their voices, you know."

"Yeah, but can they hear music?"

"They feel music."

"Then being blind would be worse because I wouldn't be able to see flowers or colors or find things on treasure hunts."

"You know what I think? I think I'm lucky for what I have. I can't do gymnastics or karate, but I've learned how to do other things, like paint and draw. I might not have tried those things other-wise. I try to think positively."

"Yeah. And anyway, who knows what tomorrow will bring," Dodie said, doing her best imitation of her father.

"Hmmm. Tomorrow." Jeffrey looked up at the sky.

"What? What's wrong?"

"It's just that I could get worse instead of better."

"How?"

"The disease takes over. It could go from my legs to my arms or anywhere else."

"But are you getting worse now?"

"Not worse, really." Jeffrey looked away again. "I'm staying pretty much the same, I guess."

After a long while Dodie said, "I really meant all those things I said before. About being sorry."

"I know. I can tell. I always know whether somebody's telling the truth or not. A lot of people will smile at me or try to have a conversation, but I know it's fake. They're just spectators. Rubber-neckers, I call them." He looked over at Dodie. "You were a rubbernecker at first."

Dodie's head filled with excuses. They buzzed around in her brain and jumbled her thoughts.

"I thought I was—I mean, I tried to—no, you're right. I was just trying to get a good look. But only because I wanted to be friends."

"That's OK. Everybody does it sometimes."

"Do other people ask you questions all the time like I do?"

"I don't think anybody asks as many questions as you do, Dodie." Jeffrey laughed.

"I know. I can't help it. I just seem to wonder about things all the time. Don't you?"

"Of course," said Jeffrey. "You know what I always wonder about?"

"What?"

"Well, it usually happens when I'm painting. I wonder, how did colors get to be colors? I mean, how did blue get invented? Or green? Or yellow? Did somebody just take the colors of the sky and trees and stuff and make them into paint?"

"Hmmm, I never thought about that."

"And sometimes I wonder if there are other colors that haven't been invented yet. I mean, totally new colors, not just what you get when you mix two or three together, but ones that could be made by some magic process."

"You could be a scientist!"

"I always thought I would invent something."

"You kind of already do, with your artwork. You create something every time you draw. Isn't that like inventing?"

"Yeah, I guess it is."

Jeffrey reached around to the back of his chair.

He fished inside a special pocket his mother had sewn on. "I finished this today." He held out a drawing.

Dodie looked at it for a long time. "Wow. That's a really cool scene. It looks sort of fuzzy."

"I did it with pastel brights."

Dodie studied the drawing. It was another one of a faraway land. An enchanted forest early in the morning, kind of misty and light. Dodie had the feeling that if she looked more closely there would be little creatures peeking out at her through the leaves and mist. But she didn't see any.

"How did you do that?"

"Do what?" Jeffrey grinned.

"Make it seem like there are people or something hidden in the picture."

"It's how I felt when I drew it. I felt like there should be fairies or elves playing tricks or dancing back there. But I didn't want to show them."

"That's so cool. Do you think everybody can see it that way?"

"Only if they believe in magic."

"Wow. I wish I could do that when I make up songs. Put something extra in."

"How do you make up a song?" Jeffrey asked.

"Well, sometimes I just start out humming or whistling, and then I add words about whatever

I'm doing at the time, and it turns into a song. If I really like it, I write it down."

"How do you know if you like it? How do you know if it's really good?"

"I don't know. I guess it just feels right to me, in my heart or something. Like I want to keep singing the song over and over again, really loud."

"I know what you mean. My mother calls that 'inspired.'"

"My brother, Peter, calls it getting on his nerves."

"He doesn't like music?"

"He does. He just doesn't like mine, I guess."

"You'll have to try it out on me sometime. Maybe you could even teach me a song." He looked at her sideways. "But no shows."

"OK." She smiled. "No shows."

"Do you want this?" Jeffrey held out the drawing.

"Really? I can have it?"

"Yeah, it's a present."

# Chapter **Twelve**

"**M**om, look what Jeffrey gave me!" Dodie ran into the house, waving the drawing. Her mother was sitting on the living room couch, leafing through an old book.

"Wow. It's beautiful, Dodie. He made that?"

"Yep! What are you looking at?"

Dodie's mother showed her the cover of her high school yearbook. "Want to see?"

"Yeah." Dodie set Jeffrey's drawing down carefully on the coffee table. Then she sat next to her mother on the couch.

"Here. I'll show you a picture of Dad." Her mom flipped through some pages and then pointed.

"That was Dad?" Dodie was looking at a teenage boy with a skinny face and long hair.

"Yep. And here's me."

"Why did everybody have such long, stringy hair?"

"It wasn't that stringy. That was the style back then. Look. Here's another picture of your father." Her mother pointed to the same skinny boy, surrounded by a bunch of smiling, goofy faces.

"Why are you looking at your yearbook, Mom?"

"Oh, I don't know. It was just out, and your father picked it up and started flipping through it."

"Was Dad here a long time?"

"A little while."

"How long?"

"I don't know. Why?"

"Just wondering." Dodie kept her eyes on the book. "What did you guys talk about?"

"I don't know. Just stuff. You sure are curious today, Dodie."

"I'm curious every day, in case you haven't noticed. It's what makes a person intelligent."

"Oh, I've noticed, all right."

Her mother continued to look through the yearbook, smiling.

"Hey, Mom? I told Dad we're doing OK without him."

Her mother's smile dropped to the floor. "And what did he say to that?"

"Not too much. But I think it made him nervous."

"Nervous? Your father?"

"Well, surprised. He seemed surprised."

"And what made you tell him that, anyway?"

"I don't know. We were just talking about why he moved out and all that."

"Let me get this straight," said her mother. "You and Daddy were talking about our separation?"

"Yeah."

Dodie's mother looked puzzled. Finally she said, "So do you want to ask me any questions about it? Or do you understand everything now?"

"Well, not everything."

"What don't you get?"

"Well, why is love so complicated?"

Her mother laughed and kissed the top of her head. "As soon as I figure *that* out, honey, I'll let you know."

Dodie stood up. "Can I look through your medical books?"

Her mother stared at her. "I don't think you'll find anything about love in there!"

"No. Not about that. It's a question about Jeffrey."

"Oh, I see. Sure."

Dodie sat down at her mother's desk. A group of big books stood upright between two bookends. Dodie turned her head sideways to look at the titles.

"That big red one is probably the easiest," her mother said. Dodie pulled it out and started flipping through the pages.

"Muscle . . . Muscular . . . Muscular dystrophy. Here it is." Dodie read silently for a few minutes. Then she turned toward her mother.

"Mom? What does *atrophy* mean?"

"It's when something loses all its strength and power because it's not getting used enough."

Dodie continued to read to herself. "It says here that when muscles atrophy, the body turns to fat in that place. Oh. That's why Jeffrey has such chubby legs." Dodie read on.

"Mom? This book says that most people with muscular dystrophy die before they turn twenty. And it also says that sometimes they get really sick in the end. Is that all true?"

"Yeah, I'm afraid it is."

Dodie sat with the open book on her lap. "But why, Ma? Why? Why do bad things have to happen all the time?" Dodie put the book away and went to sit next to her mother.

Her mother reached out to hold her hand. "I don't know, sweetie. It's just life, I guess."

"Well, I hate it. It's not fair. He's just starting to be my friend."

Dodie leaned her head on her mother's shoulder. She stayed there for a long time. Her mother stroked her hair. Finally Dodie sat up and sighed. "Well, Jeffrey's only eleven years old. He still might have a long time to live. And in the meantime, maybe they'll find a cure for his disease. Do you think it could happen?"

"Maybe. It's a hard disease, though. Doctors have been looking for a cure for a long time, and they still haven't found one. It would probably take a miracle."

"A miracle? You mean like magic?"

"Well, more like a gift from God."

Dodie knew her mother believed in God. But they didn't talk about Him much. Or Her. Or It. Whatever God was. Her mother said what God looked like didn't matter. The important thing was to know that God existed. Everywhere, in everything, and in everybody. Dodie couldn't tell if she felt God in her life yet or not.

She thought for a long time. She stood up and stretched. Finally she said, "Ma? How do miracles happen?"

Her mother was smiling over her yearbook again. "Oh, I don't know. Some people say you can pray for them. You know, ask God for help."

"Did you ever pray for a miracle?"

Her mother smiled. "Well, I prayed for you—and look, here you are!"

"Hmmm. Well, I think the worst part of all this is that Jeffrey knows. He knows what could happen. How does a person go through life knowing he could die at any time? I don't get it."

"You probably get used to it and just accept it. Maybe you just keep hoping."

Dodie shrugged. "Yeah, I guess so."

She went up to her room and flopped onto her bed. She flicked the radio on and started humming along. She sang the words without thinking. She stared at the ceiling. She turned over onto her stomach. Then she lay on her side. Suddenly, something her mother had said jolted her out of bed.

She got up and ran to the kitchen. She started rummaging through drawers. She mumbled to herself, "I know we must have some somewhere." She picked through old broken toys, screws, a shoe brush, and some bent safety pins till she found what she was looking for—candles. "These will work, I think."

Next she pulled a chair up to the refrigerator and felt around on top. She turned to make sure nobody was around, then she swiped a book of matches and jumped down to the floor. She carefully replaced the chair and ran back to her room.

Probably her mother was napping by now. Dodie stopped by her bedroom door. It was open a crack. "Ma?" she called softly. No response. Dodie opened the door a little farther. Her mother lay sleeping, her magazine facedown across her stomach. Dodie pulled the door closed and tiptoed back to her own room.

She locked her door and pulled the shades down. She sat on her bed and laid the candles and the matches out before her. Then she looked around the room for something to use as a candleholder. She spied the little milk-carton plant she had tried to grow at school. The plant had never come up, but the carton still sat on her windowsill, full of dirt.

Dodie got down on the floor. She remembered that people knelt when they prayed. She knelt, but the floor felt awfully hard. She knew that in some churches they had a special cushion to kneel on, so she grabbed her pillow from her bed and slipped it under her knees. Then she stuck a candle into the dirt in the milk carton. She struck a match and tried to light the candle, but it wouldn't light. She tried two more times.

"What are these, expired or something?" She grabbed the box they came in and read the label.

"*Get laughs with no-light candles!*" They were Peter's trick birthday candles. She sighed and threw the box down. "Ha ha." She knelt again.

She whispered, "Dear God . . ." Her voice sounded so strange. She talked to herself all the time, but this was different. Did people pray out loud or silently? Did it matter? She tried again, this time mouthing the words. "Please let Jeffrey get better." She closed her eyes and clasped her hands in front of her chest. Then she sat back and leaned against the bed.

# Chapter **Thirteen**

**D**odie couldn't wait to see Jeffrey the next day and find out if her wish had come true. She ran to his house and sneaked around to the back porch. She pushed her face up against the screen and made a shield around her eyes. She watched him as he read the Sunday comics.

"Boo!" she shouted.

"Hey! You scared me. I practically jumped out of my seat."

Dodie swung the door wide open and ran inside. "Really? You almost did?" she asked breathlessly.

"Almost did what? Jump out of my seat?"

Dodie nodded, her head bobbing wildly.

Jeffrey raised his eyebrows. "I don't think so. That would be some miracle, huh!"

Dodie slumped down in a chair. "Yeah, well, it was a thought."

Jeffrey eyed Dodie. "What's up with you? You came in all happy, and now you look kind of mad."

"Nothing. I mean . . . I was just thinking . . . Never mind. Can I have the other part of the funnies?"

"Yeah, sure." Jeffrey looked at Dodie out of the corner of his eye. "They're over there."

Dodie walked back home a little while later. She stopped to pick some flowers for her mother.

"Thanks, Dodie!" her mother said, kissing her on the forehead. "How did you know that's just what I needed?"

"I don't know. I just knew."

Her mother smiled and got out a vase to put the flowers in.

"Mom? Remember yesterday when you told me about miracles? You said that if you pray for them, they happen."

"I didn't say that they *always* happen. I said sometimes they do."

"Yeah, well, I prayed for something and it didn't come true. Why not?"

"Well, praying is kind of like letting go of a balloon. You set it free and hope that it will be found."

"But what if it isn't? How will you know?"

"You won't. But it makes you happy just to let it go, doesn't it?"

Dodie thought for a long time. "But Mom? What if the balloon pops?"

"It might. Some things just aren't meant to be."

"Well, that kind of ruins the whole idea, doesn't it? Why pray if it might not come true?"

"Why let a balloon go if it might pop?"

"But it might not."

"Exactly. Here." Her mother patted the kitchen table. "Come help me arrange these flowers, and try not to worry so much."

# Chapter **Fourteen**

"**D**o you like to bake cookies?" Dodie asked Jeffrey. They were sitting on Jeffrey's patio drinking lemonade, enjoying the sunshine.

"I don't know. I never really did it before, I guess, other than watching my mom. Do you?"

"Yeah, especially chocolate chip cookies. Mmm. Hey. I have an idea. Why don't we go to my house and make some right now?"

Dodie and Jeffrey had spent every afternoon that week together, doing homework, sitting outside, or throwing a Frisbee back and forth. Dodie hadn't had to join the after-school program. Her mother liked her spending time with Jeffrey instead. But they never went to Dodie's house. It was much easier for her to come to Jeffrey's, where things were set up for "wheelchair living," as he called it.

"OK. But wait. How are we going to get my chair inside?"

"Don't worry. We'll find a way. Our back door is like yours. It's close to the ground. Come on."

"Well, I don't know. I should at least tell my mother where I'm going."

"So tell her. I'll wait for you."

Jeffrey hesitated. Then he said, "Oh, never mind. I'll just call her from your house if I need to. She knows I'm always with you anyway."

At Dodie's house, they struggled a bit getting Jeffrey's chair to fit through the doorway, but finally Dodie got him inside her kitchen.

"I'm glad you're not any bigger," she joked.

"Yeah, me too."

While Jeffrey watched, Dodie rummaged through cabinets and drawers, pulling out all the cooking utensils they would need.

"Dodie! Do you have to make all that noise?" her brother called up from the basement.

"Oh, excu-u-u-se me. I guess you're on the phone with one of your pukey girlfriends and we've disturbed you," she shouted back sarcastically.

Peter started up the stairs. "It just so happens that I'm doing homework. Something you've probably never heard of." He paused when he saw Jeffrey. "Oh, hi, Jeff. How's it going?"

Dodie mimicked Peter's words silently behind his back, making faces.

"Dodie, why do you guys have to play in the kitchen, anyway?"

"We're not playing. I want to teach Jeffrey the cooking show."

"Oh, boy. I bet he can't wait for that."

"Well, for your information, Jeffrey doesn't know how to bake cookies, so I'm going to show him how."

"Why don't you teach him how to make a rump roast? 'Yes, that's right, ladies and gentlemen. You'll love this rump roast. You'll never leave any behind!'" Peter nearly fell on the floor laughing at his own joke. Jeffrey laughed, too, but Dodie wasn't listening anymore. She was busy taking out mixing bowls and baking pans.

"Dodie, did you forget?" Peter said. "Mom said I'm supposed to be in charge of the kitchen when she's not here."

Dodie rolled her eyes. "Yeah, but couldn't you do your homework in the dining room so you could still keep an eye on us?"

Peter stroked his chin. "Let's see. You already owe me your next allowance. We could add a couple bucks onto that . . ."

"Come on, please? I've made cookies before. I know how to do it."

"OK. But don't make a big mess."

She turned back to Jeffrey. "All right. Now, where were we? Oh yeah. See, Jeffrey, when you do the show, you have to explain everything to the people in TV land. For example, I'll measure out a cup of flour and then tell the audience what I'm doing. Watch. 'And so, folks, use one cup— no more, no less—to get the right texture.'" She lumped a pile of flour into a measuring cup.

"Wait. What are we making?"

"Jeffrey, I told you. We're making chocolate chip cookies."

"Oh, then don't we need to tell the audience that?"

"Yeah. I'll explain everything, and you just do what I'm saying, OK?"

"OK."

"First you need to beat the eggs a little before you put them into the batter."

"What batter?"

"The batter for the cookies."

"All we have is one cup of flour."

"Well, if you'll just hold on for one second, I'll show you how we make the batter!" Her shoulders drooped. "Jeffrey, I thought you wanted to do this."

"I do. But you're not explaining everything."

"All *right*. Then I'll start over. 'Ladies and gentlemen, it's important to have all your ingredients on the counter before you begin to cook.'" She waved her hand over the baking supplies as if they were prizes on a game show.

"'Vanilla, brown sugar, baking soda—'"

She whipped around the kitchen, grabbing bags and boxes from cabinets and the refrigerator. She climbed onto the countertop to reach a high shelf. "I know the nuts are here somewhere . . ."

"Dodie?"

"What, Jeffrey? If you're going to say that I'm not explaining why I'm up here with my head in the cabinet, don't bother. We're going to start all over once everything is neatly laid out. OK?" When Jeffrey didn't answer, she looked over her shoulder. "OK?"

A wet spot had formed between Jeffrey's legs and was slowly creeping out onto his thighs.

Jeffrey held his face in his hands.

Dodie jumped down from the counter. "Oh," she whispered. "Are you all right? What should we do? Don't be embarrassed. I'm your friend." She touched Jeffrey's shoulder. "Do you want me to call your mom?"

"Dodie?" Peter walked into the kitchen.

Dodie scrambled to step in front of Jeffrey so Peter wouldn't see the wet spot. Too late.

"Oh, uh . . . did you have an accident, Jeffrey? That's OK." Peter tried to sound reassuring, but Dodie could tell he didn't really know what to say or do either.

Jeffrey just stared.

"I can help you get cleaned up if you want," said Peter. "Or do you want me to take you home? Or you could borrow a pair of pants, maybe. I have some old ones that will probably fit you."

"Pants, thanks," Jeffrey mumbled.

"I'll go get the pants. I can help you change in Mom's room. It's the biggest and the closest. Dodie can show you where it is."

Dodie had never felt more grateful for having a big brother like Peter than she did at this moment.

Dodie wheeled Jeffrey down the hall. She stopped at the bathroom. "Do you still have to— I mean, is it too late?"

"I'll go in." The doorway was just wide enough for Jeffrey to wheel himself through.

"But, uh, do you need any help?" asked Dodie. "Should I get Peter to lift you or something?"

Jeffrey chuckled. "You think somebody has to lift me every time? Oh, man. My mother would break her back! This is what I use." Jeffrey reached into his chair pocket and pulled out a plastic bottle with a tilted neck.

Dodie said, "Oh, I get it. It must be a lot easier that way."

"Yeah. And I can still have my privacy, too."

Dodie backed out of the bathroom. "OK. Just call me when you want to come out . . . or whatever."

When Jeffrey and Peter finally emerged from her mother's room, the boys were laughing and telling jokes. Dodie didn't know what could possibly be so funny, but she was relieved that Jeffrey seemed to be having a good time.

Dodie was stirring the cookie dough. "Here. Want some chips?" She held the bag out to Jeffrey.

He parked his chair, and Peter patted him on the shoulder. "Keep the pants, buddy." The two of them cracked up.

"What's so funny?"

"Oh, it's just that when Peter was trying to get me into them, we ripped a big hole in the rear end."

"I guess you're lucky you can sit on it and nobody will see!" Dodie joked.

"Yeah, this chair comes in handy, doesn't it?"

"Jeffrey, does that happen to you a lot?"

"What? Ripping my pants?"

"No. You know."

"That I peed in them? Well, it happened last week. But never before that."

"What does your doctor say about it? I mean, is it a big deal or anything?"

"He said I may have to start paying more attention. That I shouldn't try to hold it in."

"So it's not a big problem, then."

"No. I guess not. Can I have some more chips?"

Dodie held out the bag for him. "Just a few more. We have to save the rest for the cookies."

# Chapter **Fifteen**

**D**odie sat on her bed. She noticed Jeffrey's latest painting still sitting on her nightstand. She looked around the room for somewhere to hang it. The place was a mess. Clothes hung over chairs. Books and magazines lay open on her desk and her bed. Every surface was covered with something. She decided it was time to clean up. She went to her desk first. She organized her books and straightened up her drawers.

Then she spotted her yearbook lying on her desk. She flipped it open. Turning the pages, she suddenly remembered Brenda's picture. She picked up an eraser and tried to get rid of the mustache and glasses she had drawn earlier. *Well, she probably didn't mean to steal my place in the show,* Dodie thought. She blew away the eraser dust and put the book on a shelf.

Finally Dodie started pulling old papers down from her bulletin board to make room for Jeffrey's painting. She came across an old clipping from the "Kids' Korner" page of the newspaper. It was a poem from a weekly poetry contest she'd entered last year. She remembered how excited she'd been when she received a letter telling her she'd won that week's contest. But that was nothing compared to how she felt when she saw the poem itself in print the following week. It read:

*FALL*

*Fall is just the time of year*
*To see the summer disappear.*
*Fall is very cool, and yet*
*It's warm enough that you forget*
*That winter's coming on.*

Her family had been so proud of her. Even Peter. She decided to keep the poem tacked up. She pinned Jeffrey's painting next to it. It was a picture of him at his easel, with Dodie at the other end of the room singing a song. Anybody looking at the painting could tell she was singing because musical notes flowed out of her mouth and floated around her head. She looked silly in the drawing, her mouth wide open with that little red thing in the center of her throat showing. But she loved the picture anyhow. Just like she loved all of Jeffrey's artwork.

Right now, though, it made her feel sad. She felt sad for Jeffrey's weak legs. She felt sad for her own problems. She looked toward the window and noticed the birthday candle sticking up out of the milk carton. "I hope you're listening, God, wherever you are." She stared at Jeffrey's picture some more and thought hard. She traced the painting lightly with her fingernail. *Jeffrey is such a good artist,* she thought. She wondered if he had ever entered a contest or exhibited his artwork in a show. He would definitely win something if he did.

She stared at the picture some more and then smiled. *Hey! Maybe . . . maybe . . . that's it! What a great idea!*

# Chapter **Sixteen**

"**I**'ll be right back!" Dodie called as she raced out the door. Shoes slapping on the pavement, she ran the entire way to Jeffrey's house.

"Jeff! Jeff!" she said, panting, when she finally got to his art studio. He was cleaning some brushes and putting things away.

"Hi, Dodie."

"I have a great idea."

"Another great idea? I'm still drying out from your last one."

"Har har. No, seriously—just listen first before you say no. All right?"

"OK. Go ahead."

"Well, I was sitting in my room looking through my stuff, trying to find a place to hang your latest work of art." She smiled at him. "And I thought, I'm good at singing, and Jeffrey's good at art . . ."

"And?"

"Well, I thought, what if I made up a song for your spring show and you painted a mural to go with it? I could sing the song, with the mural in the background. That way we could be in the show together, but you wouldn't even have to appear onstage! So, what do you think?" She held her breath and waited for his reply.

"I don't know," Jeffrey said. "It sounds kinda weird."

It wasn't the response Dodie was hoping for, but at least he hadn't said no yet. "It's not weird! Different, maybe. But not weird!"

"I'm not sure the audience would get it."

"Yes they would, if the song and the picture really went together."

"But what would they be about?" asked Jeffrey.

"They could be about anything." Dodie thought for a moment. "How about friendship? I could write a song about the importance of friends, and you could paint scenes of the two of us doing things together to show what friends do."

Jeffrey didn't say anything.

"Oh, come on, Jeffrey, *please?*"

"All right . . . I guess we could give it a try."

"Yippee!" Dodie jumped up and hugged him. "Thank you, thank you, thank you!"

"Oh, brother. You don't have to get all 'kittens and babies' on me. I'm still not sure this is gonna work."

"It'll work—I know it will!" She didn't care if he had some doubts. She was sure it would be a hit.

"Well, we better get started right away, then. We only have three weeks before the show," Jeffrey said.

"Now you're talking!"

They began to make plans and discuss different ideas. They decided not to tell anyone what their act was going to be, so it would be a surprise when people saw it.

They continued working on the plan until Dodie's brother appeared at the door. "Dodie! Mom didn't even know where you were! It's time to come home."

"Oh, sorry. Guess I lost track of time." She shook Jeffrey's hand as she was leaving. "Remember, it's a secret, right?"

Jeffrey shook back. "Yup. Just between us."

# Chapter **Seventeen**

**A**ll Dodie could think about for the next few days was the show. On Tuesday, as she sat in music class, she worked on her song in her head. Except that she had no song. Now that she was trying, her mind seemed to go blank. While the other kids shrieked and shrilled on their little plastic recorders, Dodie hummed to herself, trying to come up with her own tune. Miss Platz glared over at her, and Dodie quickly turned her mind back to "Frère Jacques."

At three o'clock she dragged herself to the cafeteria for Scouts. She was the last to arrive. She saw the troop leader setting up for today's project. *Oh, great,* Dodie thought as she plunked down her backpack. *We're making things out of soap. Again.*

Dodie was fed up. When her mother had asked her at the beginning of the school year if she wanted to be a Scout, she had said yes right away, thinking it would mean things like cooking over a campfire and sleeping in a tent. But this group never so much as went outside for a nature walk.

Dodie excused herself to go to the girls' room. She wasted some time wandering around the halls. She looked at all the bulletin boards. She stared out the windows. She peeked into the kindergarten. She smiled at the scribbly drawings posted on the door. As she examined the baby pictures the little kids had brought from home, Dodie heard music.

She stopped to listen. Someone was playing the piano. The person was playing loudly and with a lot of feeling, making each note come out strong and clear. Dodie didn't think she'd ever heard such happy music before. It made her want to dance.

She walked down the hall and poked her head into the music room. It was Miss Platz. Of course— Dodie knew she played the piano. She had just never heard her playing it this way before. Dodie couldn't help tapping her toes to the beat as she listened.

So lost in her own music was Miss Platz that she didn't even notice Dodie standing there. Finally

Miss Platz finished playing and sat back. Dodie was about to walk away when her teacher looked up.

"Dodie? Is that you? You can come in if you like."

Dodie hesitated in the doorway. "I liked that song you were playing."

Miss Platz seemed surprised. "Oh, really? Thanks. It's my latest composition."

"You mean, you made that up?"

"Yes. It's not quite finished, though. It still needs some polishing."

"Well, it sounded good to me!"

"I'm glad you liked it." Miss Platz fidgeted with her glasses and finally rested them on the end of her nose. "You know, Dodie, I can see that you really like music, but for some reason you don't seem to like it in my class."

Dodie blushed.

"I guess it puzzles me and, well, makes me feel a little bad when you don't follow along with the rest of the group. Do you think you could tell me what the problem is?"

"Well, I like to sing . . ."

Miss Platz peered at her.

"And the recorder is OK, too . . ."

"But?"

"What I really like is making up my own songs."

Miss Platz smiled. "Ah, I see."

"Sometimes I hear my own music when I'm supposed to be playing with the group."

"That would make it hard to follow along."

Dodie nodded.

"Would you like to play some of your own music right now?" Miss Platz asked.

"I don't know." Dodie suddenly felt shy in front of her teacher.

Miss Platz waved toward the closet. "Help yourself to a recorder. I need to practice a bit more." She turned back to the piano.

Dodie walked to the closet where the instruments were kept. Miss Platz started playing her song again from the beginning. Dodie stood and listened once more to the sounds that floated out to her. She closed her eyes. Soon she found herself tapping her feet and playing air-piano, moving her fingers up and down an imaginary keyboard as she tried to imitate what her teacher was playing.

Miss Platz stopped and looked up. "Would you like to sit over here while I play?"

"OK." Dodie pulled up a little round stool next to Miss Platz. Her teacher began to play once more. Dodie noticed that Miss Platz changed the music a little this time. She jazzed it up by adding notes and changing the tempo a bit. One minute Miss Platz belted out the notes, her fingers racing back and forth. The next minute she slowed down, letting the notes flow out softly. It still sounded like the same song, but Miss Platz was experimenting with the beat and the melody. Dodie noticed Miss Platz humming to herself. She seemed to be singing the notes almost before she played them, as if that helped her know what key to play next.

When Miss Platz was finished, Dodie said, "Do you want to hear the song I'm making up?"

"Sure."

"Well, it's just the beginning."

"That's OK."

"I didn't write it down or anything yet."

"Let's just hear what you have."

Dodie hummed the tune she was working on for Jeffrey's show. "That's all I have so far," she said.

"Let's hear it again," said Miss Platz.

Dodie hummed the notes again, and then suddenly thought of a few more to add on at the end. She repeated the whole thing, a little louder. Then a new feeling came over her, and with it, words to go with the notes. She sang,

> *A friend is someone special who,*
> *when you're feeling blue,*
> *Can chase away the cloudy skies*
> *and make the sun shine through.*

Then she stopped.

"Now let me see if I've got it." Miss Platz played the melody on the piano. Then she played it again and Dodie joined in, singing. Then Miss Platz added chords and some other notes, giving it style, like she had done with her own song.

Dodie couldn't believe it—her music on the piano. It sounded ten times better! It sounded like a real song. "Wow! I've been trying all week to figure out how that should go. Then all of a sudden it just popped out!"

"That's how music is. It's always inside you, waiting to come out. You just never know when or how it's going to come bubbling up."

"Hmm. I never thought of it like that."

"When you get stuck," continued Miss Platz, "instead of trying to force the music out, just stop and listen for a while."

"Listen to what?"

"Your feelings, or whatever's inside you. You might not hear anything at first, but be patient. Just keep your ears open, and it'll come to you when you least expect it."

"I'm not great at listening."

Miss Platz smiled. "You'll learn."

"Can we do it again?"

In response, Miss Platz played the opening chord.

When they finished, Dodie said, "I think I better write down the words so I don't forget them."

"Good idea. I'll write down the piano part, too." She looked over the top of her half-glasses. "Just in case we ever do it together again."

Miss Platz gave Dodie some blank paper and a pencil. After Dodie finished writing down the words, she practiced the tune on her recorder. Then she tried playing it in different ways— speeding it up, slowing it down, changing a few of the notes around. Experimenting with the song was fun, and easier than she had expected. There seemed to be no end to the variations she could come up with.

"You ready to go, kiddo?"

Startled by her mother's voice, Dodie nearly dropped her instrument. "Already? I just started."

"Miss Platz says you've been at it for almost forty minutes."

"Wow. I must have been dreaming. I didn't even know time was going by."

Miss Platz stood up. "Your mom was looking for you at Scouts, Dodie."

"Oh no! I forgot all about it!"

"The troop leader was looking for you, too," said Miss Platz. "She came by here, but when she saw you playing, she decided to let you stay. She said she thought you'd be happier here."

Dodie tried to hold back a smile. "They were making soap projects, Ma."

"I know. I saw all the little cat faces and hearts."

"And I was writing a song. Listen." Dodie played what she'd been practicing. "It's not finished yet."

"You made that up all by yourself?"

"Miss Platz helped me."

"Well, I encouraged you, Dodie. But the music is all your own." Her teacher adjusted the sides of her glasses and peered over the top.

"Miss Platz, I feel like you're two different people when you look over your glasses at me like that."

Her teacher let out a howl of laughter. "That's just what my sister always tells me! I guess I'm afraid I might miss something you say if I can't see you clearly when you're talking."

Dodie's mother handed Dodie her backpack. "You ready to go?"

"Yeah, now I am. Thanks, Miss Platz."

"You're welcome. If you want to come back next week, we can play together again and I can show you some more things."

"Really? Mom, can I?"

"What about Scouts?"

Dodie took a deep breath. "I don't really want to be in Scouts anymore, Mom."

"No?"

"Nah. It's kind of boring. We always do the same thing. I'd rather be working on my music."

"Well, if Miss Platz is sure she doesn't mind, then I don't mind. You're positive you won't miss doing those soap projects?" Her mother winked.

"Yeah, right," Dodie replied.

That evening, Dodie went over to Jeffrey's to play for him what she had come up with. When she got there, he was lying on the couch in the living room.

"Hi, Jeff. What's up?"

"Not much. Just resting. I'm not feeling too well."

"Oh, you have a cold or something?"

"Yeah, something like that."

Dodie slid a chair over to the couch. She took her recorder out of its pouch. "I wrote the first part of our song. You want to hear how it sounds?"

"Yeah, I guess so. But I thought you were going to sing it, not play it."

"I am going to sing it. But I learned how to play it on the recorder, too."

"Oh, that's great." Jeffrey pulled his blanket

closer to him and huddled under it.

As Dodie played the tune, she watched for Jeffrey's reaction. He closed his eyes. Probably so he could concentrate better on what he was hearing, she figured. When she was done, she asked, "So what do you think? Do you like it?"

Jeffrey slowly opened his eyes. He let out a little shiver. He adjusted the blanket over his legs. "It was nice." Then he closed his eyes again.

Dodie moved her chair closer to the couch. She could hear Jeffrey breathing very loudly. He sounded like he had asthma.

"Jeffrey? Should I sing it now? Or should I come back another time?"

"No. You can sing it. I'm just really tired. And it's hard for me to breathe sometimes. That's why I sound like this. But I can hear everything. The music makes me more relaxed."

Dodie sang the song quietly. Jeffrey's breathing became heavy and slow. When she was finished, she could see that he had fallen asleep. She stood up and whispered, "I'll see you tomorrow."

But Jeffrey did not respond.

# Chapter **Eighteen**

**D**odie waited for Jeffrey at school the next day. She hoped he would be back to his regular self so they could work on their project together. She put her books in her desk and waited. In twos and threes the kids piled in, laughing and shouting. Each time somebody entered, Dodie looked up, hoping to see Jeffrey wheel in. Finally the bell rang, with no sign of him. Dodie sank down into her seat.

She fidgeted the whole morning, tapping on her desk, rearranging her papers, and doodling on folder covers. Every time she heard someone in the hall, she sat up in her seat and tried to see who it was. But by lunchtime, Dodie knew Jeffrey wasn't coming.

During recess, she wandered around pulling up grass and throwing stones. She tried working on her song some more, but her heart wasn't really in it. And anyway, she had left her recorder at home. Finally, Dodie picked up a stick and sat down on the steps. She scratched her name into the dirt, and then scratched it away.

A shadow appeared over her.

"Hi, Dodie."

"Oh, hi, Miss Strawberry," Dodie answered without looking up.

"You writing your name there?"

"I was. Do you know where Jeffrey is today?"

"His mom called and said he wasn't feeling well."

"Yeah. I saw him last night and he seemed a little sick." Dodie scratched a tic-tac-toe game into the dirt. Miss Strawberry picked up another stick and filled in an *O*.

"Well, I think he just needs a little more rest today," Miss Strawberry said.

Dodie stopped with her stick in midair. Her mind flashed back to her mother's medical book. It had said sudden illness was a part of his disease.

"Is Jeffrey the first kid you've had in class who was in a wheelchair?"

"Yes. But I taught one girl who had a disability."

"Like Jeffrey's?"

"She had trouble walking, so she used crutches and had special braces on her legs."

Dodie swallowed hard. "Is she OK now?"

"What do you mean, 'OK'?"

"Still in school . . . not sicker . . . you know."

"I never saw her after she left our school."

A shiver ran up Dodie's back. "I hope she's all right, your old student."

Miss Strawberry straightened up. "Let's wait and see if Jeffrey comes back tomorrow."

The rest of the day, Dodie just stared out the window. Luckily Miss Strawberry didn't call on her. She couldn't concentrate on anything, and now she had a stomachache.

She rode the bus home, resting her head against the window. Suddenly she felt tired and could hardly stay awake. When the bus rounded the corner to her street, Dodie looked out and was surprised to see her mother standing at the bus stop.

"Hi, Mom! You never wait for me here anymore. Not since I was little."

Her mother hugged her hello and smiled stiffly. "I know."

Dodie looked up. "So why did you come meet me today?"

"Well, I have something to tell you." Her mother chewed her fingernail, then stroked Dodie's hair.

"What, Mom? Just tell me."

"Well, Jeffrey had to go into the hospital today."

"Why? What's wrong with him?"

"They're not exactly sure. They're monitoring him to find out. His mom wanted me to tell you."

Tears began to fill Dodie's eyes. "Did she say I could visit him?"

"We'll have to go there and see. Usually they don't let kids under fourteen in. But I know everyone on that floor. Do you want to take a ride over now?"

"Yeah, but let me get something first." Dodie ran inside the house and grabbed her recorder. She hoped they allowed musical instruments in the hospital.

As they stepped through the big sliding doors, Dodie clutched her mother's arm. She tried to breathe without sniffing the air, but even through her mouth she could still smell the bitter medicine odor and the scent of cafeteria food.

They passed by the coffee place and the gift shop. Dodie kept up a brisk pace to stay with her mother. As they walked through the halls, her mom waved to the doctors, nurses, and other people she knew.

"How can you stand working here, Mom? Doesn't it make you sick to your stomach?"

"Nah. You get used to the gross stuff pretty quickly. Especially when you know you're helping people and making them feel better. Besides, I'm usually too busy to notice."

"Whatever," Dodie mumbled.

"Are you OK?"

"I don't know. I guess I'll make it."

When they finally arrived in the pediatrics waiting room, Dodie slid into the nearest chair while her mother went to find the nurse in charge. Dodie closed her eyes and tried to relax. She heard a little kid scream. *Oh, no,* she thought. *Do I really want to be here?* Her stomach churned.

"Dodie? We can go in now. Just for a little while."

Dodie licked her lips. She wasn't sure she could get up. She braced herself against the arms of the chair and rose. "Are you sure it's all right for him to have visitors? Maybe he's too sick and we should come back tomorrow."

"We can come back tomorrow, if that's what you want. Is it?"

"No, I guess not. I'll go in now."

Jeffrey had two blankets wrapped around him even though it was a warm spring day. A clear tube stuck out of one arm and connected to a plastic bag. The bag hung on a pole standing next to him. Dodie walked toward him and stood at the foot of the bed.

"Hi, Jeff."

"Hi, Dodie. How are you?"

"I'm OK. How about you?"

"I'm just having dinner." He pointed to the tube. "Pepperoni pizza. See it going through?"

Dodie watched the liquid flowing slowly through the tube. "Eeeew, gross."

"Maybe they'll bring you a slice."

"Ha, ha. Why do you have to talk like that?"

He smiled. "I'm just kidding. I'm getting some tests done, and that's some special medicine they have to give me."

"Do they hurt, the tests?"

"Not really. They just gouge me for blood, mostly. And hook me up to machines to monitor my heart and lungs. But look at this." He held up the inside of his arm for inspection. It was all black and blue, a huge bruise. "The nurse couldn't find my vein. She had to prick me about a million times looking for it."

Dodie winced. She turned toward the door and noticed that her mother had gone out into the hall to talk with Jeffrey's mom.

Jeffrey pulled a round plastic bowl from under the covers. "Since you're here, you might as well help out." He started to hand Dodie the bowl.

Dodie automatically jumped back. "Get that bedpan away from me!"

Jeffrey cracked up. "Just kidding. It's empty. See?" He tipped it on its side.

"Man, you're really warped, you know that? And for somebody who's supposed to be sick, you don't seem all that bad."

"Well, I am, believe me. Can you plump up my pillows a little?"

She smiled. "Oh, brother. You're pushing it, Jeffrey." She walked over to the head of the bed and adjusted his pillows.

Jeffrey closed his eyes and lay back softly.

"I tried to work on our song today during recess," Dodie said, "but I couldn't get past the first part—you know, the part I played for you last night."

"Do you want to play it for me again?"

Dodie pulled the recorder out of her bag. "Do they allow music in here? It sounds so quiet." At that moment, a child howled in pain.

Jeffrey shook his head. "He's been screaming all day."

"Yeah, I think I heard him before," Dodie said. She wet her lips and began to play.

When she was done, Jeffrey said, "You play really nicely. Every time I hear it I feel like I want to sleep."

"Sleep? It's supposed to make you feel happy."

"Just because I want to sleep doesn't mean I'm not happy. When I'm in the hospital I like to sleep a lot. Then I don't have to remember that I'm sick. I can just fade away and dream about something else."

"What do you dream about?"

"All kinds of things. What it would be like to run again. What it would be like to do flips. And you know what I dream about all the time?"

"What?"

"I dream about how it would be to go on all those rides at a carnival again. Especially that one where you stand up straight and it spins around really fast and presses your body to the wall."

"That's practically my favorite one. But why can't you go on some of the other rides?"

"Well, for one thing, they never build them so I can get up on them. You almost always have to walk up steps. For another thing, it wouldn't be safe. What if there was an emergency and everybody had to get off right away? I'd be stuck."

Dodie thought for a minute. "You know what I'm going to do when I grow up? I'm going to make an amusement park just for physically challenged people. I'll have ramps everywhere and special rides that won't be dangerous, but they'll still be fun. I'll even put in special lifts, like elevators, that could carry you up to the rides."

"And I'll help you. I'll test everything out to see if kids would like it or not. Even though I'll be an adult by then, too."

Dodie held up her recorder and played another tune. "That's the carnival song."

"Did you just make that up?"

"Yeah. But I guess I had it in me for a long time."

Jeffrey was quiet for a moment. Then he said, "You know, I almost finished the mural."

"You did? Already? But we only talked about it this weekend. And I just started working on the song."

"Yeah, but we talked about a lot of our ideas and how it might look. So I just went from there. I can work really fast if I want to. And luckily I started it before I got sick."

"I can't wait to see it! The show is only seventeen days away, you know."

Dodie and Jeffrey looked at each other, and suddenly the room fell silent.

"How long do you think you'll be in here?" Dodie asked. "You'll be out way before then, right?"

"I don't really know. Maybe just a few days. It all depends on how fast I get better. I have to get rid of this cold first. It messes up my breathing."

Dodie thought about her prayers. She thought she heard a balloon popping somewhere in the distance. She sighed. "I wish I could help you get better."

"Just keep coming to visit me. That helps. And bring some new songs."

"So I can put you to sleep."

Jeffrey smiled. "It makes me feel more at home."

A nurse appeared at the door. "Time to take your temperature, Jeff."

Dodie stood up. "I'll come back tomorrow, OK?"

"Yeah, see you then."

# Chapter **Nineteen**

**A**s soon as she and her mother got back into their car, Dodie rolled the window down. She'd had enough hospital smells for one day. She rode with her head in the breeze most of the way home.

Finally she said, "So how is Jeffrey, Mom? What's the real scoop?"

Her mother stiffened. "What real scoop? He has a cold. And because of his muscular problems, he has trouble supporting his chest. That means he's having extra trouble breathing. Now he's being monitored." Her mother pretended to adjust the rearview mirror.

"He's getting worse, isn't he?"

"They don't know yet, Dodie. I'd rather not have you go around thinking that. Or telling him that."

"He knows a lot more than anybody thinks he knows. He's just trying to be positive about it."

"Well, that's one way to get better, for sure."

"Mom? How come grown-ups always want kids to tell the truth, but then they sometimes don't tell the truth to kids?"

This time Dodie's mother adjusted her side-view mirror. "What are you saying?"

"Like now. I can see that Jeffrey's worse. He knows that he's worse. Why do we have to say that we don't know what's happening?" Dodie paused. "This isn't going to be like you and Dad, is it? The way you guys never want to talk about the separation."

Her mother sighed. "I guess we do that when we don't know how to handle difficult situations."

They rode in silence for a few minutes. Finally her mother said, "I'm sorry, Dodie. I'm sorry that we haven't talked more about the separation. We just wanted to protect you. We didn't want you and Peter to carry around our problems."

"But Mom, Jeffrey's *my* friend, not yours. And Daddy moved out of *our* house. So those *are* my problems."

Her mom stared straight ahead and kept driving.

They rode for a few more minutes without talking. After a while, Dodie looked over and noticed tears rolling down her mother's cheek.

"Mom, what's wrong?"

"I don't know, Dode. I guess talking about these things brings up a lot of feelings."

"About Daddy, you mean?"

"Yeah. I just never thought that after all this time your father would want to be alone. That he would need space to get to know himself better." They pulled into their driveway. "And now Jeffrey and his illness. It's frustrating when things happen that we don't have any control over."

"But Mom, you could have control over the situation with Daddy. You and he could get help. That's what they always say in school. If something is wrong, tell somebody. Talk to somebody about it. Ask to see the counselor. So why couldn't you and Dad do that? See a counselor."

Her mother just stared.

"Maybe nobody can control Jeffrey's disease, Ma. But some things we can work out, right? Every problem has a solution—" Dodie's hand snapped up to cover her mouth. "Now I'm starting to sound just like Dad!"

At that her mother broke into laughter. "You're a chip-ette off the old block."

# Chapter **Twenty**

**D**odie sat on the couch next to Peter. "What are you watching?"

"Ah, I don't know. Wrestling comes on soon."

Dodie slumped down. "Pete, what does it mean that a person wants to know himself better?"

"I don't know. Where did you hear that?"

"That's what Mom said about Dad. That he moved out to get to know himself better."

"Really? That's what she said?"

"Yeah. But Peter, what does that mean? I don't understand how a person could be as old as Dad and not know who he is."

"I don't know, Dode. Maybe when you're a kid,

it's easier to know who you are because you haven't lived as long and you haven't done as many things. You're still doing things and learning about them. So it's less complicated. Like me, for example. I know I like computer games and watching TV and playing baseball. You know that you like music and being in shows and all that stuff. And don't forget your favorite thing"—Peter wiggled his eyebrows up and down—"Scouts."

"Yeah, right. Except that I quit yesterday."

"You did not."

"Yup, I did. I couldn't take it anymore. And anyway, I have more important things to do. Like writing music."

"Oh, yeah. How's it coming?"

"Pretty good. You want to hear it?" She fished her recorder out of her backpack.

"Well . . . I don't know." He looked at his watch. "Wrestling comes on in five minutes."

"Oh, OK." Dodie looked down at the floor. "Maybe some other time."

"No. You know what? You can play it right now. The first part of the show is always kind of stupid anyway."

"I know you don't really like my music, Pete."

"I do. It's just that . . ."

"What?"

"It's just that it gets so loud sometimes when I'm trying to concentrate or talk on the phone. You know what I mean?"

"Yeah, I guess so. Well, this one's not very loud. So here goes."

Dodie licked her lips and played her song. When she finished, she looked up.

Peter nodded slowly. "Pretty good. Pretty good."

Dodie took a bow. "I'll tell you a secret if you promise not to tell anyone."

"OK. What is it?"

"Promise?"

"Yeah, go ahead."

"You have to say, 'I promise.'"

"OK, OK. I promise. Now tell me."

"Well, you know how there's going to be a show at Jeffrey's clinic? We're in it. I'm making up a song and he painted a mural to go in the background."

"And?"

"And nothing. That's it. We just didn't want anyone to know exactly what we were doing for it."

"Oh, I get it. So everyone could be surprised when they saw it."

"Yeah."

"So am I invited?"

"Of course. And you better be there, too."

"Even if I have a big date?"

"Yeah. But I don't think that's going to happen."

"Me neither."

"Thanks for listening to my music, Pete."

"You're welcome. Thanks for telling me your secrets."

Dodie went into the kitchen and picked up the phone. She dialed her father's number.

"Hi, Dad. How are you?"

"Good, sugar. What's up?"

"Oh, not much. What's new with you, Dad?"

"Just working. Same old stuff."

"Oh."

"So how's life treating you, Dodie? Everything going OK?"

"Not really. My friend Jeffrey is in the hospital."

"Oh. That's too bad. What's wrong with him?"

"Well, I told you he has muscular dystrophy, and he can't walk. So he's already in a wheelchair. But now his disease is acting up. It does that sometimes."

"Well, this too shall pass."

"Yeah, right."

"I'm doing it again, aren't I, Dodie? Using a saying to fix everything."

"Yeah, you are."

"Well, I do believe in those little sayings, Dodie. They've helped me get through a lot of hard times."

"How? Just by saying them to yourself over and over again?"

"Yeah. And by trying to look at the positive side of things. What good does it do to look at the negative all the time? What good does it do to worry?"

"Dad, are you getting to know yourself?"

"Am I what?"

"You know, taking time out to get to know yourself better."

"Where did you ever hear something like that?"

"Oh, um . . . I don't know." Dodie heard the TV playing downstairs. "Sometimes they say it on *Oprah*."

"Hmm. Well, I guess it's true."

"So what exactly are you trying to find out?"

"Well, here's the thing, Dodie. Your mother and I got married very young. We loved each other, and we still do. But when you're that young, sometimes you don't think ahead. You can only see what's right in front of you. I never really lived a bachelor's life."

"But Dad, you're a father, not a bachelor."

"I know, honey. And I would never want to give up fatherhood."

"So, what's so special about being a bachelor,

anyway? You probably don't have anybody to play cards with or go to the movies with. Nobody to wrestle with."

Her father didn't respond.

"Nobody to kiss good night."

"It's true, Dode. You're right."

"So you must be a little lonely. I would be."

"Well, I am."

"Maybe Mom is, too."

"Did she say that?"

"Well, no, not exactly. But I just think she is. Girls can tell about these things."

"You just let me work it out with Mommy, OK?"

"OK."

"How about your friend? Should we drop by and bring him an ice cream soda?"

"That would be nice, but he has to eat only what the doctor says. Sometimes he even gets fed through a tube."

"How about a teddy bear?"

"Dad! He's eleven years old."

"So? You think he doesn't need company at night? When it's dark and everybody's gone home? You don't think he'd like a little friend to cheer him up?"

"Well, maybe. I'll think about it. I guess I could bring him one of my old stuffed animals."

"Even though he's a boy, he'd probably love it. Take it from a man of experience."

"OK, Daddy, I will. Bye."

# Chapter **Twenty-One**

"**M**om? Are you in there?" Dodie stood outside the bathroom. The scent of bubble bath drifted out from underneath the door. Her family created such different odors in there. When her father came out, the room smelled acidy and Dodie had to hold her nose before going in. When Peter finally emerged, the entire place was steamed up and smelled minty like pimple medicine. But when her mother took a bath, she filled the room with a flowery, soft scent. Dodie breathed it in.

"Dodie? You can come in if you want."

Dodie went in and sat on the toilet. Her mother

was covered in bubbles up to her neck. She relaxed against a special blow-up bath pillow.

"Ma? You know the volunteers who work at the hospital? I want to be one."

"You? I thought you hated the hospital."

"Well, I did. But since I've been visiting Jeffrey there for the past few days, I've gotten used to it. It doesn't really bother me anymore. He says I cheer him up when I visit. So I thought maybe I could visit other kids or grown-ups and cheer them up, too. Some of them might even want me to play a song for them. Jeffrey likes that."

"Well, I know that usually you have to be fourteen to work there, but I can find out. They always need volunteers to wheel around the library cart."

"I could do that."

"Then I'll check on it for you."

"OK."

Dodie's mother slid a little farther down in the tub and closed her eyes.

"Mom?" Dodie asked softly. "Can you tell me the story of my birth?" Dodie had heard the story a thousand times before, but she loved the way her mother told it. Hearing about when she was born made her feel happy and safe.

"Well, it was a cold winter night. I was lying in

bed, as big as a house. My water broke, and I knew I was ready to go. I woke your father up, and you know how hard it is to wake him up. Finally we got dressed and set out for the hospital.

"We used to have this old, old car that didn't go very fast. So your father was slapping the dashboard and saying, 'Come on, car, let's go.' And I was just praying that we'd get there in time.

"Well, we got there, and your father brought me in the emergency entrance. The nurse took one look at me and ran to get another nurse and a stretcher. They laid me on top of it and then whisked me off to the delivery room. You were born seven minutes later. I never even had time to take off my coat or boots!"

"And I came out hiney first, right?"

"That's right. You must have really wanted to get out into the world."

"And what did Dad say when he first saw me?"

"He said, 'A little girl. My little girl. Thank you, God.'"

"Did he pick me up, too?"

"Sure. You were lying on my chest, and he said he wanted to hold you. He held you a lot when you were a baby. When you cried out in the night, he used to bring you into our room."

"He doesn't still love me like that."

Her mother sat up. "Of course he does. Why would you ever say such a thing?"

"I don't know. He's just so into this bachelor stuff now. Living alone and all that."

"But that doesn't have anything to do with you."

"Why not? He's not here at home with us."

"I know, Dodie. But sometimes parents just can't get along, and one of them has to leave. But he's not leaving *you*. He still sees you and calls you. And he still takes care of you. Your father is a good father, Dodie."

"I know. But I miss him a lot. Even though I still see him on Saturdays."

"I know you do. And you know what? I miss him, too, Dodie."

"I think we should tell him to come back and live with us again. We could make the first night a celebration and have a party. What do you think?"

"I think your father has to work through this on his own first."

Dodie sighed. "If you say so." She stood up. "I'm going out now. It's too steamy in here."

# Chapter **Twenty-Two**

The next afternoon, Dodie visited Jeffrey again.

"Here, Jeff. I brought you my old teddy bear." Dodie held the stuffed animal out to him.

"Oh, thanks. She's cute. Put her here next to me."

"Don't you want to hold her?"

"I do. But I can't move my arms all that well."

Dodie tucked the bear under the covers. "I named her Dodo. I used to sleep with her when I was little."

"I haven't had a stuffed animal for a long time," Jeffrey said.

"I thought you might like to sleep with her at night. You know, when nobody's here and stuff."

"Is she fierce? She can be my watchbear."

"She's not fierce. She's a friend."

Dodie noticed that a new machine had been hooked up to Jeffrey's arm. "So how are things? How do you feel?"

"Well, like I said, I'm having trouble moving my arms. They feel so heavy."

"Is that why you have this new machine hooked up to you?"

"That's for my new treatment. They're injecting this stuff into me to see if I can get stronger."

"And is it working?"

"It takes a while to work. This machine is actually monitoring me."

"I get it. So we have to wait for a progress report."

"Yeah. In the meantime, I figure I can be one of those people who does everything with their teeth. I could paint, write, pick things up. Look."

With considerable effort, Jeffrey wiggled toward the side of his bed and bit into a magazine on the nightstand. He pulled it toward him. "See?"

"Now you're all crooked in the bed."

"Can you fix me?"

Dodie arranged Jeffrey into a straighter position.

"But really. I saw this lady on TV once," he said. "She had lost her arms, and she learned how to do everything with her feet. They showed her shopping at the grocery store, feeling melons with her toes."

"Eeewww. That's gross."

"Well, what else could she do? At least she was still able to do things for herself. Do you have any idea what it's like to have other people doing everything for you all the time? It stinks."

"I know. But didn't she get the melons all dirty? I mean, didn't the other shoppers mind?"

"Yeah, but what could they say? 'Please don't walk on the melons'?" With that, Jeffrey broke into howls of laughter.

Dodie shook her head. "I swear, nobody thinks you're funnier than you do."

"I'm just saying, there are still ways to get around and do things even if you are handicapped."

"Physically challenged, you mean."

"Same thing."

"That new treatment still has time to work. We don't know what could happen," Dodie said.

"I know, but I just thought I'd tell you about my back-up plan."

"Well, thanks for the information."

"Thanks for straightening me out."

"I don't think you could ever do *that* with your teeth." Dodie giggled.

"That's true."

"Hey, I might be doing something like this for a job," said Dodie.

"What do you mean? You want to be a nurse?"

"No, a volunteer. A candy striper. My mom's checking it out for me to see if I'm old enough."

"Wow. That's cool. If they say no, you can always come wipe away my drool and stuff."

Dodie smacked the edge of his bed. "Jeffrey!"

"Just kidding. Can't you take a joke?"

"You're always joking, Jeff."

"No I'm not." He paused. "I wanted to ask you something." Suddenly Jeffrey's voice sounded different. Dodie wasn't sure she wanted to hear what he was going to say next.

"What, Jeffrey?"

"I was thinking that since the show is getting closer, maybe you could go to my house and finish the mural."

"Me? But I can't paint."

"Yes you can."

"No I can't. My pictures always look like a five-year-old did them. Plus, I always splatter paint all over the place."

"Can't you just try?"

"But what should I paint?"

"When you see what I did, maybe you'll get some ideas. Then you can just feel your way through the rest. Remember what we talked about? It has to come from your heart."

"Oh, all right, I guess I can try. But don't blame me if I mess it all up."

"You won't."

Inside Jeffrey's studio, the mural lay spread out on the floor. Dodie sat down and stared at it. It was, without a doubt, the most awesome thing Jeffrey had ever created. She felt goose-pimply all over. Gold and silver glitter-paint outlined most of it. Bright purples and pinks gave it a happy, exciting feeling. As usual, it had a sort of faraway look.

Most of the mural was covered with scenes of Dodie and Jeffrey doing different things together. Dodie and Jeffrey laughing in his art studio. Dodie pushing Jeffrey around the school yard. The two of them sailing on some faraway ocean.

Dodie stared at the spots that hadn't been painted yet. "That's what it will be like without Jeffrey," she mumbled. "Lots of empty spaces." She shook her head. "I guess those are for me to fill in."

She put on a smock, brought some paints over to the mural, and sat down. She had to think for a long time before she could start. Jeffrey's words played over and over in her brain. *Feel it in your heart.*

With tears in her eyes, she started to paint. As she dabbed here and there, she thought of Jeffrey. Soon the colors got blurry, and she started to cry. She jabbed the paintbrush into the floor.

Tears streamed down her cheeks. She pounded the mural with her fist. Soon she was sobbing. "It's not fair! I hate this! And I hate you too, God! Nothing ever goes right!" Suddenly she stood up and kicked the palette of paint. A rainbow splashed onto the wall. Now she screamed, "I hate everybody! I'm never going to care about anybody again as long as I live!" She ran to a shelf and grabbed a container.

"Dodie?!" Jeffrey's mother came running into the room. Dodie didn't turn around. Instead she dug her nails into the plastic bottle and hurled it against the wall. Thick blue paint oozed out. Through her tears, Dodie watched the blue drip down the wall.

Jeffrey's mom shouted, "Dodie, wait—stop!" She began to cry, too, covering her mouth with her hands.

Dodie took another bottle of paint and walked toward the mural. She stopped at the edge of it. She turned to Jeffrey's mother. "It doesn't matter," Dodie said, trying to twist the top off the bottle. "Nothing matters. If Jeffrey's going to die, who cares about this mural? Who cares about anything?" she sobbed as she struggled with the top.

Jeffrey's mother held her hand out. She took the bottle, opened it, and handed it back to Dodie.

Dodie's mouth dropped open.

"It's true," Jeffrey's mother said quietly. "If Jeffrey dies, what could possibly matter anymore?" Tears rolled down her face. Dodie just stared.

Slowly, Dodie put the lid back on the paint. She sat down next to the mural. Jeffrey's mother sat down next to her. They stayed silent for a long time.

Finally, Dodie spoke. "I messed up the wall."

"I see that."

"I wasted a lot of paint, too."

"Yeah."

"I feel like I miss Jeffrey already." She started to cry again.

Jeffrey's mother put her arm around Dodie. "I know just how you feel."

"My heart is broken in pieces."

"Mine, too."

They cried for a little while in silence.

"Are you mad about the wall?" Dodie asked.

"No. I think it will come off." Jeffrey's mother handed her a paintbrush. "Here. Why don't you finish your real work while I try to clean up this mess."

Dodie took the brush. "I guess it *does* matter if I get this finished."

Jeffrey's mother nodded. "I think so."

Dodie took a deep breath and began to paint.

# Chapter **Twenty-Three**

**"I** finished the mural yesterday. It doesn't look too bad," Dodie said.

"That's great," replied Jeffrey. "So how's the song coming?"

"I'm not so sure I like what I have. Got any brilliant ideas?"

"Me? I can hardly remember songs on the radio, much less make up my own. Why don't you sing it to me, and I'll tell you what I think."

"I don't know. It seems so corny."

"Well, it probably isn't."

"OK, here goes. But don't laugh." Dodie stood up and began to sing.

*A friend is someone special who,*
  *when you're feeling blue,*
*Can chase away the cloudy skies*
  *and make the sun shine through.*

*And when you're feeling happy,*
  *a good friend comes to share*
*The laughter and the golden times,*
  *no matter when or where.*

Then she stopped. "See? It sounds so stupid."

"I don't think so," said Jeffrey. "I like it. What's so wrong with it?"

Dodie sighed and sat down. "Well, I guess it's OK, but . . . I don't know. I never thought it would be so hard to write this song."

"What do you mean? I thought you liked making up songs. And poems, too. That's what you said."

"I know. But that was just for fun. Now it's for real." She sighed again. "I guess I do like this song, but I feel like it needs more. I want to add something to it, something special that people will sing on the way out, you know? That's how I want it to be."

"Yeah, I know what you mean. Something they'll remember."

"Yeah. I guess I'm just not inspired."

"Well, you will be."

Dodie sat for a long time. Finally she said, "I guess you won't be out of here in time for the show, huh?"

"I doubt it. I don't think that treatment is working. Now I'm just feeling sick to my stomach all the time. And look at my toes." Jeffrey pulled the sheet away from one foot with his teeth.

"Could you stop it with the teeth already? You're driving me crazy!"

"You have to admit I'm pretty good at it, though."

"Yeah, yeah, yeah." Jeffrey's legs were even bigger than Dodie remembered them. They looked almost swollen. "Why is your foot all bruised?"

"It's from all the injections they've been giving me. They ran out of veins on my arms, so they had to start using my foot."

Dodie covered Jeffrey back up. "Does it hurt?"

"I guess it would if I could feel anything."

"Sorry, I forgot."

Dodie and Jeffrey sat in silence for a long time. Dodie listened to the buzz and click of the machines. Jeffrey just looked at the ceiling.

"Dodie? I'm starting to feel kind of afraid."

"You are? Why?"

"'Cause, well, you know."

"What?" Dodie's throat ached. Her heart stood

still, and all she could do was sit there and wait for him to answer.

"Do you know that a lot of people with my kind of disease die before they turn twenty?"

"You're only eleven."

"I know. But I just have a feeling. And I'm scared."

"You want me to tell you a story?"

"OK." Jeffrey smiled a crooked smile. Dodie noticed that since his disease had taken over, he had lost some control of his lips.

She moved closer to the bed. She smoothed down Jeffrey's covers. "You've got some droolies on your mouth."

"I know. It's part of my new look."

Jeffrey turned his head toward Dodie so she could wipe away the saliva. She dabbed at the corners of Jeffrey's mouth.

"Thanks, candy striper."

"*Junior* candy striper."

"What does that mean?"

"I get to push the carts around for the big girls, and they call me their assistant. Whoopee."

"You don't like it as much as you thought?"

"It's kind of like when I joined Scouts. I had been on a camping trip with my family, and I wanted to do more of that kind of stuff. But then our troop just made stupid little dolls and soap things. I feel that my talents are being wasted."

"Yeah, they should have you wiping snot and drool from all the patients. It could be a special service. Temperatures taken every four hours, unneeded wetness wiped every two."

"That's not what I mean. I just thought I would be more like a cheerer-upper person instead of someone who wheels a cart down the hall."

"You *are* a good cheerer-upper."

"Well, anyway, here's your story. Once upon a time, when my mother was pregnant with me . . ." Dodie told the story of her birth. She added a few made-up details, such as a near miss with a taxi and an almost-delivery in the hospital elevator.

". . . And my mom said that I've lived my life that way ever since. I want to do everything in a hurry. Do you think that's true?"

"You do rush sometimes. But not as much lately."

"Do you know the story of your birth?"

"No, I never thought to ask my mom." Jeffrey yawned. "Why don't you try singing the song again." He smiled. "I'm feeling sleepy." He closed his eyes.

Dodie began. But her voice cracked, and she stopped. She sat still for the longest time. She looked over at her now-sleeping friend. Tears welled up in her eyes and rolled down her cheeks. She leaned closer to Jeffrey and started singing again, very softly.

Suddenly, like a surprise waterfall, new words came pouring out of nowhere. She let them come. They flowed up from deep inside of her and spilled out like her tears, filling in the holes of the song. When no more words came, she closed her eyes and took a deep breath.

Jeffrey snored loudly. She touched his toes through the sheet and leaned down toward him. "I wish I could help you, Jeff. I really wish I could."

# Chapter **Twenty-Four**

**D**odie stood backstage, waiting to hear her name called. Her heart was thumping. She peeked out from behind the curtain. She could see Miss Platz settling down at the piano. At least that had worked out. During one of their after-school sessions, Dodie had told Miss Platz about the show, and the teacher had offered to accompany Dodie.

Now Dodie looked up to the ceiling. That's where people always seemed to look when they prayed. *Thanks for sending Miss Platz,* she said silently. *Jeffrey's not here, but at least I'm not all alone.* Then the show emcee announced her name, and the curtain pulled back to the side.

The audience oohed and aahed when they saw Jeffrey's mural. The silver and gold paint glistened under the spotlight. The bright colors shone. Pictures of Dodie and Jeffrey practically filled the stage.

The scenes Dodie had painted were not as life-like or as beautiful as the ones Jeffrey had done, but they had their own style—Dodie and Jeffrey sitting in the sun, Jeffrey holding a paintbrush in his teeth, and in the center, Dodie and Jeffrey riding the biggest roller coaster imaginable. Above the roller coaster, Dodie had painted a bunch of balloons flying in the sky. And across the top, Dodie had painted the word *FRIENDS* in giant letters.

When the audience had stopped whispering and pointing, Dodie walked up to the microphone. The lights almost blinded her.

"Uh, hi, everybody," she said, shielding her eyes and squinting. "I'm Dodie. My friend Jeffrey was supposed to be here with me. He painted this mural. The only thing is, Jeffrey's in the hospital and he couldn't come tonight."

A murmur rose from the audience.

"I'm going to sing a song I wrote about friends," Dodie continued. "It's called 'A Song for Jeffrey.' I dedicate it to him. Thank you."

She looked at Miss Platz and nodded her head. Miss Platz began. Dodie took a deep breath and began to sing.

> *He wheeled into my life one day*
> *and took me by surprise,*
> *A boy who rides while others run,*
> *but in his heart he flies.*

Her voice started out softly, then seemed to lift up, up, up till it filled the auditorium. Dodie was finally able to open her eyes all the way.

> *Jeffrey's someone special who,*
> *when I'm feeling blue,*
> *Can chase away the cloudy skies*
> *and make the sun shine through.*

Dodie looked out into the audience for the first time. She saw her brother filming with a video camera. Her parents were sitting together in the front row. They waved to her, but she didn't wave back. She had to concentrate on her music.

> *And when I'm feeling happy,*
> *Jeffrey comes to share*
> *The laughter and the golden times,*
> *no matter when or where.*

Miss Platz played on, a part of the music that she

had written herself. Dodie liked it and had asked her to play it just before the last verse. She took a deep breath and finished the song.

*We dream some dreams together,*
*  we dream some dreams apart.*
*He'll be my friend forever,*
*  'cause he lives inside my heart.*

At this point Dodie's voice got wobbly. She felt sad for Jeffrey. She felt sad for herself. She felt sad for all the problems her mother and father were having. Most of all, she felt sad for all the things that could not, would not last forever. She saw Jeffrey in her mind. She smiled to keep from crying as she repeated the last two lines.

*He'll be my friend forever,*
*  'cause he lives inside my heart.*

*He'll be my friend forever,*
*  'cause he lives inside my heart.*

Dodie put the microphone back on the stand. The audience cheered loudly, whistling and clapping. Some people were even standing. Dodie took a bow. And now she waved to her mother and father. She couldn't be sure, but she thought she saw the two of them holding hands. Peter had come right up to the edge of the stage and was now filming her up close. Dodie waved into the video camera. Finally, the curtain closed.

# Chapter **Twenty-Five**

"**H**i, Jeffrey. You awake?"

"Yeah, sorta. Wow. Look at that outfit." Jeffrey squinted. "Pretty wild."

Dodie twirled around in a circle. "Like it?" She was still dressed in her costume from the performance. She wore a black bodysuit and tights under a chartreuse vest. The vest, from the hips down, was made of fringe. She had a large green bandanna knotted around her waist, and around her neck she wore her mother's feathery scarf.

"My mother didn't want to let me wear the vest. She wanted me to wear a skirt, but I begged."

"Cool. So how did it go?"

"I've got a surprise for you."

"You got me a vest, too, so we can be twins?"

"Funny. No, look." She held up the videotape Peter had made.

"You taped it? Let me see."

"Wait, I'll go get everybody else. Both our families are here. They don't usually let this many visitors in at the same time, but luckily my mom was able to pull some strings."

"Oh, that's great. Tell them to come in."

Jeffrey's parents, Dodie's parents, and Peter all paraded in at once, waving and talking to Jeffrey. Mostly they were telling him how wonderful the mural looked. His mother and father had brought it all the way over from the show so Jeffrey could see it.

When everybody was situated around the room, Dodie popped the tape into the VCR. At first the images jumped up and down. A shot of someone's head appeared, then suddenly a foot filled the screen. "It's all bouncy, Peter! What were you doing, jogging or something?" Dodie teased.

"It gets better, squirt. Just watch."

Dodie rolled her eyes. "I hope so. I feel seasick." In truth, Dodie was thrilled that her big brother had thought to tape the show for her. He had borrowed the camera from one of his friends as a surprise.

Dodie sat next to Jeffrey. As the tape played, he pointed out who his friends were from physical therapy. Dodie and Jeffrey giggled and whispered together about the various costumes and performances. Finally, after some skips and some more bouncing in the tape, Dodie appeared on the screen.

Everybody in the room watched her performance in silence, then clapped when it was over. Jeffrey's father went out to get some sodas. Somebody suggested they watch Dodie again. Peter got busy rewinding the tape.

Next to her, Jeffrey asked quietly, "Were those the same words you sang to me the other day?"

"Well, mostly. Some new ideas came to me at the last minute."

"I really liked them. But I feel kind of embarrassed that you sang about me. I thought the song would be more about us together."

"Well, it is about us together. It's just from my point of view."

Jeffrey smiled. "I'm glad you got a tape of it. Hey, thanks, Peter."

"No problem. By the way, they loved your mural, in case you couldn't tell by all the applause. Not to mention all the people who came backstage afterward to get a closer look."

"I'm glad. I don't think I'll be painting another one for a while."

Dodie looked down at the floor.

Peter started the tape again. Jeffrey's father came back with the drinks. Dodie looked over at her parents. They were smiling at each other and seemed unaware of anyone else in the room. She nudged Jeffrey. "Look at my parents," she whispered.

"They're in love."

"You think so?"

"Yup. You know how you can tell? Your mom's makeup is smudged around the eyes, and she has a piece of food or something stuck in her front teeth, and she doesn't even know it."

"She looks kind of funny, doesn't she?"

"Yeah. But your father doesn't think so."

Dodie looked over at them again. She opened her mouth wide and pretended to stick her finger down her throat.

"Hey, you wanted them to get back together, didn't you?"

"Yes, but I didn't think it would be like this."

"Didn't they used to love each other like that before?" Jeffrey asked.

"I don't know. All I remember is the fighting. And anyway, since when did you become such an expert about love?"

Jeffrey blushed and said nothing.

Then his eyes filled up with tears. "You know, you're my best friend. Except for the kids at the clinic, nobody else ever took the time to get to know me like you have. Nobody else visited me here. Nobody else brought me presents and sang to me." Now tears were rolling down his cheeks. Dodie untied her bandanna and wiped them away.

"Thanks," he sniffled. "I guess I'm just an invalid now, huh?"

"You still have your teeth."

Peter started the video again. Soon Dodie heard Jeffrey's labored breathing. She knew without looking that he had fallen asleep.

# Chapter **Twenty-Six**

The next Saturday, Dodie's father took Dodie and Peter out together. They went to the arcade first. While Peter was off playing video games, Dodie and her father played pinball.

"Dad? I think I saw you and Mom holding hands at my show."

In the blinking lights of the pinball game, Dodie saw her father blush. He kept his eyes on the game and pressed the flippers quickly. The ball slipped through the center and disappeared.

Without looking up, her dad said, "Oh, really?"

"You were! I knew it! Are you trying to psych me out or what?"

"No. You're right. We were holding hands."

"Does that mean you don't want to be a bachelor anymore?"

"Oh, I don't know, Dode."

Dodie rolled her eyes. "Then what *does* it mean? Holding hands. Why do you and Mom have to keep everything a secret?"

"We're not keeping secrets. We just want to be sure about things before we make any big decisions. Sometimes people feel a certain way about each other, but that doesn't mean all their problems are solved."

Dodie pulled back on the pinball spring to release a new ball into the game. It shot around the top of the machine, then bumped down and around the pathways. As it ricocheted from side to side, bells rang and points registered with a click, click. Dodie watched but couldn't respond in time when the ball rolled down the slant of the flipper. It disappeared down the hole.

"But what about love? I thought love was supposed to fix everything. And whatever happened to your famous saying, 'Two heads are better than one'?"

Her father sighed. "Well, that's still true, and love *can* fix a lot of things. But it takes time. It takes a lot of trust and sometimes hard work."

"Dad, this isn't just another one of your sayings, is it? Just a way to end the conversation without really explaining anything? I mean, what kind of work are you talking about?"

"You know, like being patient and accepting. Trying to love someone, even when that person is totally driving you crazy."

Dodie thought for a minute. "Oh, then it's just like being friends. Sometimes I want to strangle Jeffrey when he won't do what I want. And you know what? Even now that Jeffrey is really sick, I still get mad at him. I even get angry that he's so sick and can't come out and do things. But then I feel bad because I know he can't help it."

"That's natural. People have their feelings even when somebody is sick."

Dodie was silent for a while. The pinball machine buzzed. "Daddy? What am I going to do if Jeffrey doesn't . . . doesn't . . . I mean, if he dies?"

Her father reached out and took her hand in both of his. "We'll work on that when the time comes."

"But everything is so much work! I had to work hard to get him to be my friend. I have to work hard to be his friend while he's sick. And now I might lose him and I *still* have to work at it!" She leaned against her father and started to cry. "It's not fair. I just want things to go my way for once."

Her father put his arm around her, and they walked to a place in the corner where they could sit.

Dodie just sat there, leaning against her father for a long time. Finally she sat up. "And I don't want you to be a bachelor anymore. I want you to come back and live with us."

"We'll see. Let's take it one day at a time, OK?"

"'We'll see' usually means no."

"This time it means that we have to wait until we find out what's best for everybody before we make a decision."

"I hate waiting."

Her father stroked her hair. "I know. It's one of the things that makes you you." He smiled and kissed the top of her head.

Dodie rolled her eyes and leaned into the crook of her father's arm. "I know that must be some kind of a compliment."

Her father hugged her and stood up. "Listen, I have to go call the office."

Dodie sat up. "Right now? On a Saturday?"

"I'll be back in two minutes."

Dodie sighed and watched him walk off into the crowd. She mumbled to herself, "Well, I guess 'we'll see' is better than nothing." She got up and went to look for Peter. She found him still playing the same video game.

"I just won my third free game in a row! Can you believe it?"

"Wow. That's great. Can you stop after this one? I'm hungry."

"OK. Let me just get a couple thousand more points."

"Pete? Did you ever feel really sad? Just sad about everything?"

The machine buzzed loudly. "Dodie, I'm concentrating! What kind of a question is that, anyway?"

"I don't know. I just feel so bad lately that I'm not even in the mood to do anything."

Finally Peter finished playing. He leaned close to Dodie and put a brotherly arm on her shoulder. She leaned away from him. "Your armpits stink. Did you put your deodorant on today?"

"Thanks a lot, Dodie! Try to have some sensitivity for a guy. I just got done playing about twenty kabillion games of Sonic."

"You still smell. You're not going to get a girlfriend that way."

Peter pretended to grab her around the neck in a fake wrestling move. "—And Vinnie the Vice-Grip Malone goes for the headlock!" he shouted, jumping up and landing with an exaggerated thud.

"Yeah, right. Like wrestling is almost going to make me feel better."

"Just trying to have a little fun. Wow. You *are* in a bad mood."

"That's what I'm trying to tell you! It's not easy being me."

"Come on. Let's go find Dad and get some pizza. That usually cheers you up." Her brother put his arm around her again. This time Dodie felt comforted by the weight of it on her shoulder. "It'll be OK," he said. "I'm pretty sure you won't always feel like you do now."

Dodie looked up at her big brother. "I guess your armpits don't smell that bad after all."

Their father was walking toward them.

"Hi, Dad," Dodie said. "We're ready for some pizza now."

# Chapter **Twenty-Seven**

**A**t the hospital, Jeffrey was propped up in bed, watching TV. Dodie hadn't seen him in a couple of days. She had thought that staying away would help prepare her for when he was no longer around. "Out of sight, out of mind," her father used to say.

Only it worked in reverse this time. The less she saw Jeffrey, the more she wanted to see him. Dodie had learned a saying for that, too: "Absence makes the heart grow fonder." Staying away hadn't made anything better. Jeffrey was sicker than ever, and she still couldn't get used to the idea of him not being around anymore.

"Hi, Jeffrey. How's it going?" she asked, coming through the doorway.

He didn't look up. "Just terrific. I played tennis this morning, and I have a karate class tonight. In between, I'm going to run a few miles." His expression didn't change.

Dodie stopped and stood still. There was a sharp edge in Jeffrey's voice that she hadn't heard in a long time. "What's up with you?"

"What do you mean, what's up with me? I can't get out of bed, I practically pee on myself every day, I hate staying here, and you ask what's up with me. I hate everything! I'd throw something if I could. But I can't even do that."

"Did something happen?"

"No, nothing happened. I'm just sick of being in bed all the time while everybody else is out there doing fun things."

Dodie wasn't used to Jeffrey talking like this. She didn't know if she should leave or stay or try to make him laugh or tell him everything was going to be all right. She opted for going over to the bed and taking his hand.

"I know I probably don't understand *exactly* how you feel, but I think maybe I can imagine it a little."

"No, you can't! Nobody can! My life stinks! I wish I was dead already!"

A chill went through Dodie. This she could relate to. Still holding his hand, she said, "I can imagine wanting to be dead. You know, there were times when I thought I wanted to die, too. Like when I found out my father was leaving our family. Or when my grandmother died when I was little. I felt like my whole life was over. Is that how you feel?"

Jeffrey sniffed. "Yeah, I'm just really mad that I can't get better!"

"Is there anything that would make you feel any better at all?"

Jeffrey shook his head. He closed his eyes and mumbled something.

"Do you just want to be alone?"

He sighed and turned his head toward the wall.

Dodie stood up slowly. "I guess I'll come back later, then."

Dodie took the elevator to the main floor. Her mother wouldn't be picking her up for another twenty minutes. She wandered past the gift shop and looked at the items in the window.

In the center sat a vase filled with artificial flowers. No matter what other items were on sale that week, these same flowers were always part of the display. A price tag hung from one dusty green leaf. Ten dollars had been crossed out. Then $5.00. Now the flowers cost $2.50. Something about the way they stood, stiff and lifeless, depressed her. No patient would ever want those, Dodie thought as she walked away.

She passed the coffee shop. The smell of fried food drifted out to her. She loved french fries, but today the odor made her feel sick to her stomach.

She hurried down the corridor and found herself at the hospital chapel. She had walked past this room dozens of times before, never giving it a second thought. But now she opened the heavy padded door and peeked inside.

She tiptoed in, letting the door close quietly behind her. As her eyes adjusted to the darkness, she looked around the empty room. Something about the place felt familiar. It reminded her of her grandmother's funeral. The chapel didn't really look like the funeral home, but both places were dark and hushed, and the floors were covered with the same thick carpeting. And there was something else that Dodie recognized—a feeling. She couldn't quite put her finger on it, but she knew she felt it.

The chapel didn't look much like a church. There were no candles or crosses. There were no colorful windows. In fact, the room was very plain, with a long table up front and a few flowers placed here and there. Church or not, though, it seemed to Dodie like a place where you could talk to God.

She slid into a chair and sat down. She wasn't sure how to pray here. She didn't know if there were any special procedures she should follow. Did she have to cross herself or bow or ask a special beginning question so God would know it was her calling from a strange place? She had knelt on a pillow at home. Was she supposed to kneel here, too?

Finally she decided that it didn't matter where she was or how she did it. If God was real, He or She or whatever God was would hear Dodie's prayers no matter what. Standing, sitting, or on her knees.

She took a deep breath and closed her eyes. She thought for a long time. Mostly she thought about Jeffrey and his angry feelings about dying. She didn't blame him. She was angry, too. It didn't make sense to her. Why should a boy—not even a teenager yet—get a disease? Why should anybody get diseases, or for that matter, die?

As she questioned God in her mind, an image came to her. It was of one of Jeffrey's paintings, the first one she had ever seen. The one with mist and clouds in the background and waves rolling by, all purply and blue. But in this version, she could see Jeffrey in the picture. He was in a boat on the water. And the funny thing was, he was *standing* in it, as if he'd been standing all his life!

He was singing something that sounded like an old pirate song:

> *O-o-o . . . O-o-o-me-o.*
> *Well, blow me down and shiver me timbers,*
> *I'm a long way out and I want to go home.*

Over and over he sang, "I want to go home." He had his eyes closed, but he was smiling. The way he looked was totally unlike the way she had just seen him, upstairs in the hospital bed. For one thing, he looked lighter, as if he were actually floating above the boat. For another thing, he looked calm and restful, not pale and weighed down by his heavy body. And not in pain.

But where was she getting this image from? Dodie had never seen Jeffrey standing before. So was God putting pictures into her mind? Was this heaven? A shiver ran up her back. She closed her eyes tighter and started to cry. Even though she prayed for Jeffrey to get better, she knew it was too late.

# Chapter **Twenty-Eight**

**D**odie went back to the hospital that night.

"Hi, Jeff. I brought something to show you." Dodie held up a photo album. "Wanna see?"

Jeffrey nodded.

Dodie stood close to his bed and placed the album upright on his stomach. She opened the book and began turning pages for him, since he could no longer move his arms. "See? That's me when I was little. Then there I am again. And there's Peter."

"You guys used to look a lot alike."

"I know. Good thing we don't anymore. I think I lucked out in that department!"

Jeffrey started to laugh. Then it turned into a cough. Dodie automatically reached out and covered his mouth with a tissue.

She continued to turn the pages. "There's me when I was a baby."

"Oh, that reminds me," Jeffrey wheezed. "I have something to show you. Here." He pointed his chin toward a notebook on the nightstand. "Open it."

Dodie put the album down and took the notebook. She read, "'The story of Jeffrey's birth.'" She looked up and smiled.

"I had my mother write it down for me," he said.

Dodie began reading aloud. "'One summer, our family was on vacation at Lake Winnebago. My mom was pregnant with me. My father and my uncle were fishing. My mom and my aunt were working in the kitchen, and my mom started to get really bad pains. I wasn't supposed to be born for another six weeks or so. But the pains got worse and worse. Finally my mother went to the hospital. They had to cut her belly open and take me out.'"

Dodie paused. "Her belly?" she asked.

"Yeah, it's called a cesarean section. Sometimes they have to do it that way."

Dodie continued reading. "'I was too small to go home, so they had to put me in a special case where they kept me warm all the time.'" She stopped again.

"An incubator—like how we hatched the chicks at school?"

"I'm not exactly a chick, and I didn't get hatched from an egg, either. At least not that kind."

"I know that. Hey, there's a picture of you in the incubator. You were cute." Dodie read on. "'I only weighed three pounds. My lungs hadn't expanded yet, and I couldn't breathe right.'" *Just like now,* she thought. "'The doctors told my mom there wasn't much chance of me living. I had to stay in the incubator for a whole month. Nobody could hug me or even pick me up.'"

Dodie asked, "Not even the nurses?"

Jeffrey shook his head. "Nobody."

"Well, I'm sure they hugged you a lot afterward to make up for it."

Jeffrey nodded.

"So let's see what happened next." Dodie turned the page. "'I started to grow, and finally one night before I was ready to go home, my mom took me out of the incubator and fed me.'" Dodie paused. "She must have been so happy then."

Jeffrey smiled his crooked smile.

They were both quiet for a long time. Finally Dodie said, "You must have really struggled to stay alive. Your lungs didn't work right, and you were so small, but you still managed to keep going."

"Yeah, it was almost like a miracle."

Dodie stared at Jeffrey. "Do you believe in stuff like that?"

"Well, something kept me alive. And I'm glad. I wouldn't know my parents or you or anybody if I hadn't kept going."

Dodie's eyes filled with tears. She and Jeffrey were both silent again.

Finally Jeffrey spoke. "You know, I'm scared. I'm really scared about what's going to happen to me." He lay still with his eyes closed. "Dodie? What do you think happens when you die? I mean anybody, not just me."

Dodie stared out the window for a while. "I don't know. But do we have to think about that right now? Can't we think about other things? Here. Let's look at the album some more." She thrust it toward him. She turned a few pages. Jeffrey still had his eyes closed. "Jeffrey, are you even looking?"

"What if it's really awful? I mean, like, what if there are spiderwebs and dirt in the coffin?"

Dodie sighed. "I don't know. Don't worry about it," she said, trying to change the subject.

"But what if bugs and worms—"

"Look, Jeffrey." She shoved the book closer to his face. "There's me with my underwear on my head!"

"Dodie? What if a rat chewed a hole in my coffin and got inside with me?" Jeffrey started to cry.

Slowly Dodie closed the photo album and put it down. She sat on the edge of Jeffrey's bed and took his hand. "Jeffrey? I wasn't going to tell you this, but I guess it's time now."

Jeffrey opened his eyes.

"I think I saw you in heaven," she continued.

"What do you mean?"

"I was praying, and I saw a picture of you. And you were really happy."

Jeffrey's eyes grew wide. "For real?"

"Yeah."

"And what did it look like? Where was I? Were my parents with me?"

Dodie told Jeffrey what she had seen.

"And I was standing? Are you sure?"

"Sure I'm sure."

"But you've never even seen me stand."

"I know. That's why I thought it must be heaven."

The two of them stared at each other for the longest time.

Finally, Jeffrey spoke. "I feel like going there now. I feel like giving up on this world."

"You didn't give up when you were a baby."

"I know. But I didn't know myself when I was a baby. And now I do. I've tried so hard to get better.

I kept my arms strong for as long as I could. I stayed in school as long as I could. I'm tired. And everything is so much work."

"I don't know what I'll do without you, Jeffrey." Now Dodie started to cry again.

"You'll find another friend to take my place."

"But nobody could. Nobody's just like you. Nobody's as funny or as smart or as nice as you."

"And nobody can move things with their teeth like I do." Jeffrey smiled at her sideways.

Dodie sniffled. Then she giggled. Then she reached over and hugged Jeffrey tightly.

Jeffrey couldn't hug back, but Dodie felt a warmth coming from her friend that she had never felt before.

*Dear Mark,*
*Thanks for your interest in my book. It's no Cider House Rules, but it was fun writing it. I hope you like. reads it. Love, Constance*

Meet the Author

# Constance M. Foland

*At age 11*

*Today*

**A**s a girl, Constance Foland loved making up her own songs and playing them on the recorder. She also sang in the school chorus. Today she lives in New York City, where she teaches elementary school and takes dance lessons. She still enjoys composing songs, like the ones she wrote for *A Song for Jeffrey.* Sometimes she even dreams up new songs in her sleep!